AIROVALE

Airovale

JEF GRAY

CONTENTS

AIROVALE

TIME IS THE ONLY TREASURE

Jef Gray

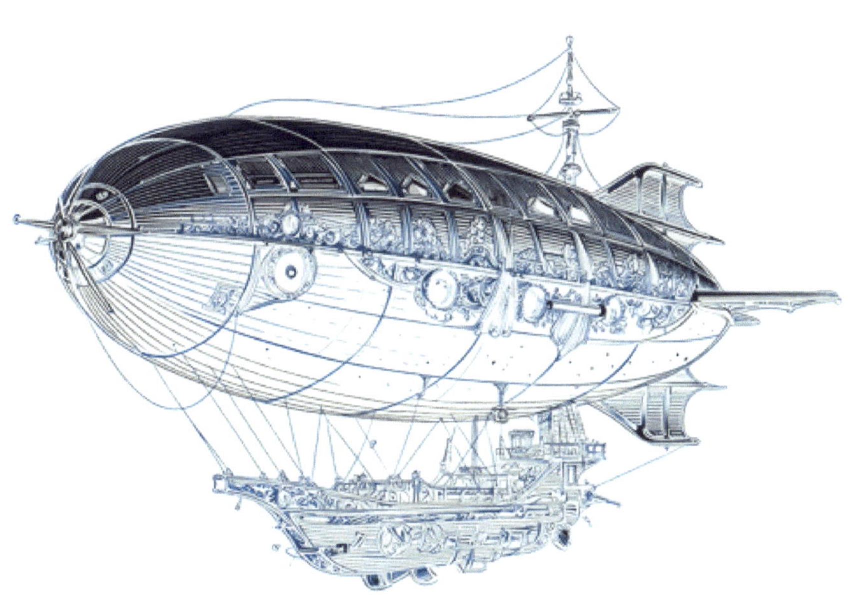

Legal

This is a work of fiction. All characters, events, places, and organizations portrayed in this book are either the product of the author's imagination or used fictitiously. Any resemblance to actual persons, living or dead, events, or locales is entirely coincidental. All text and images are the exclusive property of the author. No part of this book, including illustrations, may be reproduced, distributed, or transmitted in any form or by any means: electronic, mechanical, photocopying, recording, or otherwise without prior written permission from the author, except in the case of brief quotations used in reviews or critical articles.
All rights reserved.
Visit Airovale.com for enhanced content, including the cinematic micro-films and soundtrack based on the book.
Copyright 2026, Aurous Publishing, Inc.

Time is the only treasure,
There is no measure,
What you will give,
What you will trade,
To go back and live one single day.

Dedication

For my children.

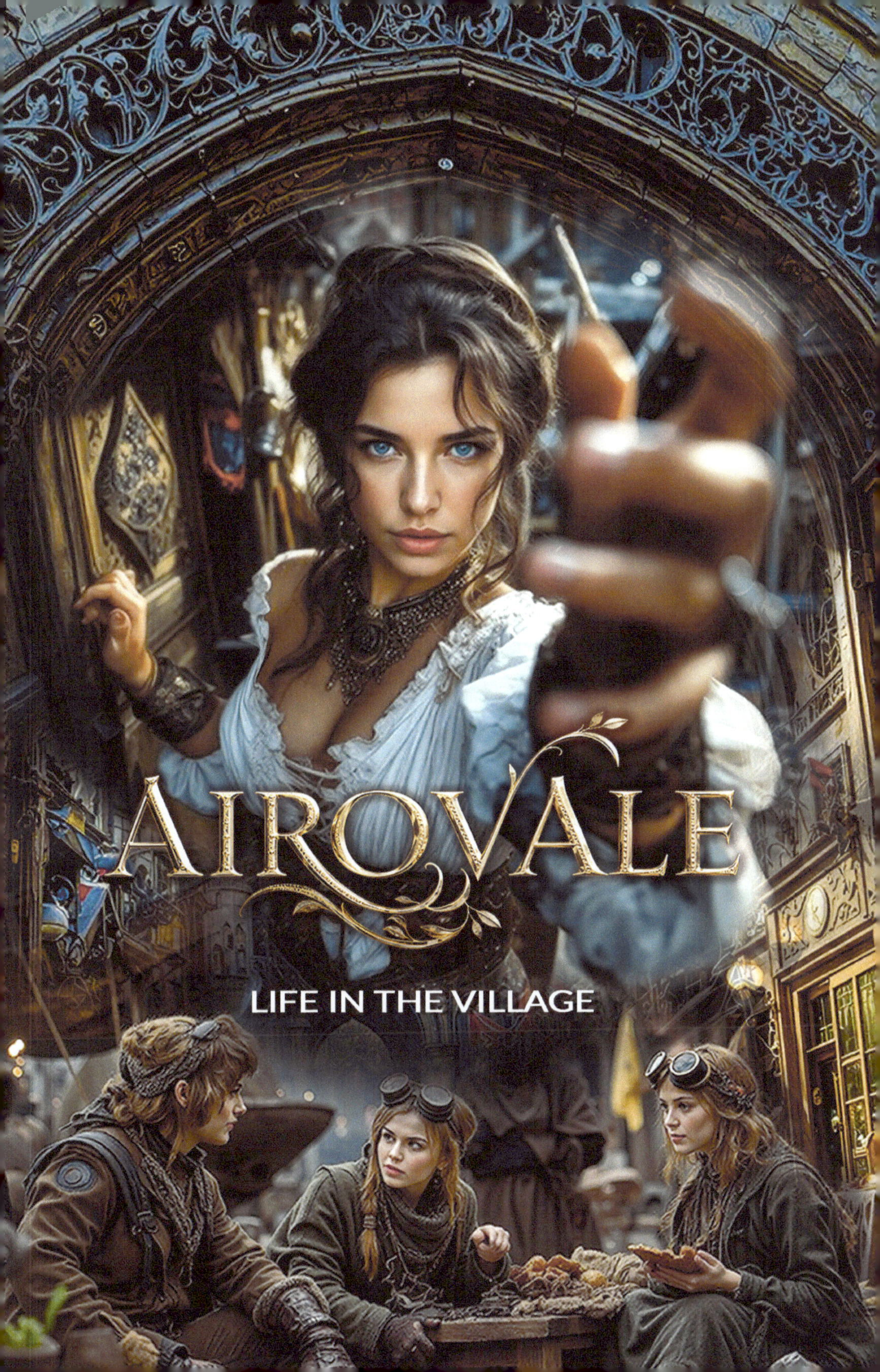

AIROVALE
LIFE IN THE VILLAGE

Life in the Village

The Gift

The gates of Airovale stretched open as morning spilled across the cobbled streets. A rush of scents met the tide of travelers—sweet apples stacked in wicker baskets, the sharp tang of salt-fish packed in ice, and the bitter undertone of coal smoke rising from the forges. Merchants called from their stalls, voices overlapping like a chorus: hawking spices, cookery, bolts of muslin and silk dyed in crimson, mint, and ivory, and leather gloves for the hands of pilots. Incense drifted lazily between the stalls, carried by the wind.

Among the crowd, Aden, a gaunt young man, paused as Kateryna, a farmer's daughter, watched him from behind her basket. Her braids were threaded with wildflowers, her eyes steady as she recognized the look of hunger on his face. It was the same look her family had worn before they found shelter in the village. Others passed her stall, coins clinking, but she held back her hand until he drew near. Only then did she press an apple into his palm, her fingers lingering just long enough for him to hear her quiet words.

"На добро," she whispered—na dobro—for good.

He blinked, unsettled by the depth in her eyes, uncertain whether she offered blessing or bargain. She smiled briefly, knowing the unseen weight kindness could set in motion, then turned away. Aden nodded in thanks, slipped the apple into his pocket, and disappeared into the press of bodies.

The Tower

High above, the groan of rigging and the hiss of escaping steam signaled the arrival of another zeppelin. Painted in blue and copper, the ship descended toward the seaport. Ropes were thrown down to the dock tower where workers scrambled to catch them. Boots clattered on the planks, shouts rose above the wind, and smoke rolled in waves as coal was loaded into the belly of the ship. The air itself seemed alive with motion—an orchestra of industry, ambition, and smoke.

From a lofted office overlooking the docks, Elara leaned out of her wide window, letting the wind toss strands of blonde hair across her face. She recorded the ship's arrival in her ledger with brisk, deliberate strokes. Every tower, every docking fee, every outbound cargo: her father's fortune and the city's order depended on it. Her father, the town quartermaster, had once done this work himself. Now he passed the legacy to her, while keeping watch from his windowed perch above the harbor.

From the tower's interior, the city's noise softened into a distant hum. Elara closed the ledger and rubbed her fingers, ink-stained and stiff. Noon bells rang from the lower districts, their tones drifting up through the open windows. Ships had departed or docked for the day, taking on provisions or unloading freight. Everything would be still now—until evening.

"Come eat," her father said.

Garrick Vale set plates of fish and vegetables on a narrow table by the window, pulling out a chair for her.

"Fresh tomatoes," he added, nodding at the dish. "Kateryna says they're the last of the season. Look at the size of them!"

Elara exhaled, numbers still ticking through her mind, and joined him, setting the ledger aside. "Five arrivals before noon," she said. "Twelve departing at dusk—if the winds hold."

Garrick tore the bread cleanly, offering her the larger half without looking. "They always think the wind will hold. You logged the Crescent traffic?"

"Yes."

"And did you mark them honest?" he asked mildly.

She hesitated. "I marked them as they declared themselves."

A low chuckle escaped him. "Good answer. Clever."

"You always say that."

"And you always prove me right." His gaze drifted back to the docks. "They don't go for copper, Elara. Not truly. Copper is what they tell their wives."

"And the Crescents?" she asked.

Garrick chewed slowly. "The Crescents are dangerous and take more than they give. They always have. I flew them before you were born—we all came back lighter in the hold and heavier in debt, those that made it back."

She frowned. "You never told me that."

"I didn't want to poison your thoughts about ambition, but trade works on a balance. If all you see is one side of the scale, you could be in deeper than you know with no way to right the measure." He met her gaze. "The wisdom is knowing when to count coin—and when to count life."

Elara followed his eyes to the streets below, where traders laughed and apprentices hurried past with bowls of stew. "One day," she said quietly, "I want to chart more than arrivals and fees. I want to own the airships. Make the trades."

Garrick smiled—not indulgently, but with something like pride. "Careful. That's how you end up like me. Chasing the wind. Always another port, another bargain. No home you ever stay long enough to miss."

The thought stilled him. For a moment, his eyes softened, drawn inward—to a woman who had surprised him with a daughter, and in doing so, taught him what treasure truly was.

"I don't mind watching," Elara said, gently breaking the silence. "Someone has to track who left—and who didn't come back. But there has to be more than keeping score in someone else's game. And I know you'll say family... but I'm not ready for that."

Garrick heard his younger self in her voice—the same hunger, the same restlessness that had once driven him skyward.

"No one is ever ready, not really. But when I landed on the field that day, and there she was, holding you..."

He placed his hand on her shoulder, looking out at the skyline. His silence became the most vivid description, as neither spoke, in mutual reflection of a wife and mother they'd lost.

Malina's Promise

Outside, a sparrow perched for a moment on the tower roof before darting toward the forest beyond the village gates, where the market's noise faded, and the cemetery lay quiet.

Malina walked its narrow paths each morning, her steps measured, her breath steady by habit alone. Dew clung to the stone markers, beading like tears that never dried. She paused before three headstones, their names carved deep, the dates staggered across decades measured in memories rather than time.

The newest stone still smelled of fresh-cut rock.

She knelt, fingers brushing away fallen leaves. "I'm sorry," she whispered—not for his death, but for surviving it.

Once, grief had been sharp. Then it became familiar. Now it was heavy, settled, like the red scarf at her throat—a garment she could no longer remove. She had buried them all with the same steady hands that had healed strangers, delivered children, closed the eyes of the dying. Each farewell had taken something from her that never returned, consuming her with a sense of void and loss.

"I won't do it again," she said to the stones. "I won't outlive another love."

The wind stirred the length of her cloak as she rose. From here she could hear the city waking fully—laughter, shouting, the clatter of industry. Life, impatient and indifferent.

That was when the thought came. Not as madness. Not as rage. But as clarity.

An end did not need to be violent or by her own hand; it only needed to be final.

Malina turned back toward the market, toward the aeronauts who chased horizons and believed fate could be outrun. The frail, ancient map was already folded within her sleeve, its weight slight, its consequence immense.

If the world insisted on motion, then she would set it moving—one last time.

She walked slowly back to the village as colors of the late afternoon market deepened into shadows stretching long across the stone streets. A breeze announced the surrender of the day's heat, as fog wove a web of glowing mist, anchored to each awakening lantern in the dimming distance.

Jonas Merrow paced in front of her shop, waiting for her to return. She noticed him as she turned the corner, a man dressed in aeronaut clothing, with an anxious face.

He saw Malina walking toward the door and interrupted her as she turned her key to go inside.

"Are you her? The seer, the...healer?" He said abruptly, inviting himself inside.

"It is late sir, and I am tired. Come back tomorrow." Malina stood by the door, holding it open.

"I will be gone tomorrow, I need something for my wife, tonight, please... I can pay!" he insisted, pouring coins nervously onto the counter where her herbs and tinctures were arranged.

"What ailment does she have?" Malina's voice softened while walking around the counter.

"She becomes ill when we fly north, the magnetic sea has some kind of effect like...", Jonas paused as he looked up from the counter.

Malina stood still, her piercing blue eyes pushed through him. Reading him, as he felt his balance shift.

"So, your wife gets airsick?"

Jonas paused, "Well, sometimes I might, also…"

"You can get ginger candy at any shop in the square." She sighed, "Why are you here?"

Jonas hesitated, his words jumbled as he tried to explain his concern, "I've heard you can see things about people, their fate…"

"You wish to know about the hidden gold in the Crescents." Malina cut in, "You and every treasure seeker that comes through here."

She slammed a bag of ginger on top of his coins, pushing them all back to him except one. "Chew one nugget before meals, and one before bed, happy hunting."

Jonas lifted the bag and put it in his pocket, leaving the coins, "I meant no offense. I just… ever since we lost the baby, this journey has been the only thing she gets excited about. If we return empty, I don't know what to try next."

Malina's hand stilled on the doorknob.

"Sorry about your loss," she said, the words hollow even as she spoke them. "They say it gets better with time, and we all have the same destiny in the end."

Jonas stood silent for a moment, processing her words, as he nodded his head and walked out the door.

Malina closed the door quickly, turning the lock quickly as her eyes welled with tears. Her face tensing as she drew a sudden breath, repulsed by the callous empty platitudes she had said, the same she had been told repeatedly.

"Time doesn't make it better, it tortures."

Riches Await

Elara pushed her window shutters back to capture the planned departures of the day's airships.

As she opened her ledger, she saw a fluttering poster on the market square wall:

VOYAGE TO THE CRESCENT ISLANDS RICHES AWAIT

She rolled her eyes in disgust, knowing the danger was not disclosed to those foolish enough to board the ships.

A gust of wind tore the poster from its nail, sending it skittering across the plaza until it caught in the tavern door. A moment later, laughter rolled from within, tumbling into the night air.

The fire roared in the tavern hearth, painting the rafters with dancing shadows. A brash youth in oil-stained leather leaned back on his stool, sloshing ale as he spoke.

"One voyage to the Crescents," Tomas declared, grinning wide, "and I'll buy a mansion for me and my five wives."

His friends jeered and raised their mugs, laughter breaking loud and uneven. Someone thumped the table in agreement.

Behind the bar, Lysa, flame-haired and sharp-eyed, set down the next round without comment. Her curls caught the lamplight as she leaned just far enough to quiet them. The bravado wilted at once. They argued over who might win her favor, showering her with compliments, though she'd heard it all before. To her, their advances were like foam sliding down their mugs—bright for a moment, then dissolved into air.

The tavern door swung wide, laughter spilling into the street.

Outside, lamplighters touched flame to glass, and the glow caught the faces of young aeronaut apprentices hunched over steaming bowls of stew. Goggles pushed up onto their foreheads, jackets creaking as they leaned in close, voices echoing in shouts and laughter.

"My uncle says the Crescents eat ships," muttered Perrin, his hair in tufts from a day under a helmet.

"Your uncle's afraid of his own shadow," Joss shot back, wiping bread on his sleeve. "All I know is the copper's real. I've seen the ingots."

"Everyone's seen something," said Marek, older than the others, quieter. His spoon paused midair. "The hard part is crossing the magnetic sea."

Their voices lowered after that—as if admitting fear made them unwise. This was their last meal in Airovale before the ships carried them toward the unknown.

One of them pointed toward the hangar, where sparks burst like fireflies as crews hammered steel ribs into a new zeppelin hull. The clang of iron on iron echoed into the night.

"That's where my ship will be built when I return with the gold!" Joss announced confidently.

Airovale was more than a capital city—it was the forge of flight. Zeppelins were crafted and commissioned from its port every year by generations of skilled engineers and craftsmen.

On nearby crates stacked high with supplies, older aeronauts argued as they strapped down their gear.

"If I find that temple," said Rusk, a broad-shouldered pilot with scarred knuckles, "I'll carry back more treasure than a man could spend in ten lifetimes."

"It's cursed," replied Anya, perched on a crate beside him, coiling rope with practiced ease. She lowered her voice as though the shadows might overhear. "That temple's guarded by an old witch."

Rusk snorted. "That's just a legend. Fear will keep you poor. Besides, I've got a map to where it's hidden."

Anya shot him a sideways look. "Rusk! Everyone's got a map—they sell them to tourists."

Their voices drifted down the street and into the dark, where Malina stood listening.

The Burden

She stepped through the crowd of aeronauts, cargo handlers, and family members as each ship prepared to launch. Her eyes caught a pilot adjusting his gloves at the edge of the street. His coat was well kept, his posture careful—too careful for a man about to wager his life.

Jonas Merrow startled as she stepped near and slipped a folded parchment into his pocket, her fingers closing briefly around his wrist.

"All treasures are a burden to bear," she whispered, low enough for only him to hear.

Jonas quickly patted his pockets, thinking he had been robbed. He paused in relief, then looked toward the woman waiting a few paces away—Sabina Merrow, his wife. Her gaze already fixed on him, sharp and expectant. She did not ask what the stranger had given him. She only raised an eyebrow, as if reminding him that hesitation was a luxury they could not afford.

Jonas swallowed, nodding once to himself. When he turned back, Malina was already gone—swallowed by the crowd.

His hand brushed the frail parchment tucked inside his coat. He drew it out briefly, studying the tattered edges, the faded markings, the ancient script naming the islands. A chill passed over him, sharper than the night air.

"Jonas?" Sabina said insistently.

He folded the map again and slipped it deep into his jacket. "Coming," he replied, though his voice betrayed him.

Sabina smiled—thin, satisfied. "Good," she said. "Then let's not be late."

Moments later, their zeppelin, the *Gilded Star*, rose from its moorings and drifted into the dusky sky.

Na Dobro

The rising airship's glow washed across the square, churning with noise and light as lanterns swung in the evening breeze. A gust tore through, scattering scraps of parchment and the smell of coal smoke.

Aden stood beneath the loading ramp of a large grey zeppelin. His jacket was threadbare, his boots worn thin, his face dirty after weeks in the jailhouse where he'd been sent for stealing from the markets. Hunger had made him a thief, though in his mind the greater crime was starving. An orphan of the streets, he had been hardened by want and alley fights, learning early to risk everything for a chance at more than only surviving.

He walked toward the jubilant sounds of the tavern, slowing as he noticed a boy crouched in the shadows, his face hollow with hunger. The sight struck him like a memory—of alleys, cold nights, and the ache that had once gnawed at him without mercy.

Aden reached into his pocket and found the apple, its skin still warm from the hand that had given it. For a moment he hesitated as this was the only food he had, then he knelt and pressed it into the boy's palms. The child's eyes widened, a smile breaking through the grime.

"Na dobro," Aden whispered to himself.

The wind caught a stray poster and slapped it against the wall above them.

VOYAGE TO THE CRESCENT ISLANDS RICHES AWAIT

The boy bit into the fruit, juice running down his chin. Aden looked up at the words, the promise of fortune pulling at him like a tide. When the paper tore free and skittered down the street, he followed, his steps carrying him toward the last ship taking on crew.

The *Nereid* loomed before him, its hull grey with age, ropes creaking as the crew loaded coal and cargo. Aden squared his shoulders and stepped forward.

A salt-marked veteran towered over the gangplank. Captain Von Holt squinted at Aden as he approached.

"You look poor," the officer said. "What use are you to me? Ever cut your hands on stone? Ever been chased by old Aelmir above the clouds?"

"No, sir," Aden answered, his gaze steady. "But I can dig. I can hunt. And if it comes to it—I can fight."

The captain studied him, then smiled faintly. "You'll shovel coal by day and hunt when we dock. Fail in either, you'll be left behind. Do it well, and you'll take an equal crew's share. Understood?"

"Yes, Captain."

Turning, Von Holt shouted up the gangplank, "Get him some clothes—and a meal!"

Laughter and compliance rang out from above. The captain motioned to move along, and Aden boarded—the first time he stepped onto a ship as crew, not stowaway.

Come Back to Me

Along the field of tethered ships, another zeppelin, the *Ironwind*, prepared to rise. A rugged man stood apart, holding his beloved in a long embrace.

"When I return," he promised, "I'll be a rich man. Then we'll marry, and you'll never want for anything again."

"First Mate Kael! Time to push off!" the captain called.

"Coming, Captain!" Kael replied.

Mira trembled in his arms. "You are my treasure, Kael." She sighed as he stepped up the gangplank.

"Come back to me," she whispered in her heart as the *Ironwind* lifted from the field, swallowed by the fog and bound for the Crescent Islands.

Time and Treasure

From the quartermaster's tower, Elara noted the last ships to depart, her pencil moving slower now as twilight settled over the docks. Below them, lanterns bobbed like fallen stars as crews cast off lines and lovers clung a moment longer than they should.

Garrick stood behind her, pipe in hand, watching each vessel disappear into the haze. His gaze lingered longer than the rest, as if willing one of them to turn back.

"They always look the same at this hour," he said quietly.

Elara glanced back at him. "The ships?"

"The promises," he replied.

She returned her gaze to the sky as one zeppelin tilted into the wind. "They believe in what's waiting for them."

Garrick exhaled a thin ribbon of smoke. "So did I."

Elara hesitated, then set the pencil down. "Do you regret your life as an aeronaut?"

He considered the question longer than she expected. "No," he said at last. "But I didn't see what it cost."

He nodded toward the departing lights. "I thought time was mine to keep. One more season. Another voyage. I'll come home later." His voice lowered. "Later was a lie I told myself—and her."

Elara's throat tightened. She had never heard him speak of her mother like this.

"All those men tonight," Garrick continued, "making promises and leaving to chase riches far away, while their real treasure waits at home. And if a man stays, how does he provide?" He shook his head. "That's the paradox—how to live without always exchanging time for money."

Elara swallowed. "But you did come home."

Garrick smiled—not sadly, but with a gentleness shaped by loss. "Becoming quartermaster was the only way I could be here when your mother fell ill."

He met her eyes. "And once I was, I saw how much I'd missed. Those few years before she was gone were worth more than every journey I ever made."

Elara stood and embraced her father as the distant sound of engines faded.

The Wish

Below, in the square, Malina drew her shawl close and lifted her hands, palms open to the night. Words left her lips—old syllables shaped by longing for those who live no more.

The prayer caught in her throat, her hands shaking to overcome the doubt in her mind.

"Have I asked too much in this life, or am I punished for lacking the courage to demand more?"

A whirling wind of smoke and leaves began to center around her, as if listening and weighing her wish.

She spoke in pale misty breaths, "Let the map reveal what none can find, and the gold that cursed no longer bind."

The wind held for a heartbeat—then scattered.

She watched until the glowing hulls of the fleet blended with the stars. It was no longer her burden to guard the map or decide the fate of who held it.

The Crescent Islands awaited.

AIROVALE
THE CRESCENT ISLANDS

The Crescent Islands

Arrival at the Crescents

Rows of zeppelins appeared on the horizon, lumbering in from the magnetic sea before sunset. They came in mismatched lines—freighters with patched canvas and scarred plates, small traders strung with sails, lean vessels that looked fast even at a crawl. Officially, they were here to mine copper in the caves. In truth, every ship among them had a second hunger: discovery of the temple gold.

The voyage had taken two weeks across water where compasses spun like toys and blue lightning flashed in a clear sky. Along the way, some turned back, blaming wind or sickness, but fear of going down was the ultimate struggle. Their ropes twisted at odd angles. Needles jittered. Somewhere in the rigging men swore they heard a laugh. They called the passage Aelmir's Span—the storm-bearded giant's realm, where the wind could turn a ship inside out without warning. Those who pressed on now beheld the Crescents at last: curving volcanic spines clawing from the sea, canyons clouded with perpetual fog, and rivers cutting deeper each season into a hidden basin of lush greenery, markets, and treacherous caves.

On arrival, every ship had the same priority: provisions. Two weeks aloft had emptied their supplies and rationed their water to sips per day. The ships descended on canyon markets with urgency to take on supplies and continue onward to their mining sites before losing daylight.

On the cliff farms, girls worked the terraces with long-handled tools, the skirts of their dresses brushing rows of cabbage and beans. At the far edge of the fields, they paused and shaded their eyes, watching shadows wheel across the sky. They did not wave; to them, zeppelins meant empty larders by nightfall and trouble by dawn—ale gone to froth, and laughter that overstayed its welcome in the taverns.

As the *Ironwind* dipped into the canyon, one of the farmgirls plucked a lemon from a branch and hurled it over to a passing deckhand. It arced against a pale cloud and fell, caught by his calloused hand. The aeronaut appeared grateful.

"That's a sour welcome," said Kael.

"No, I think she likes me," said the young apprentice as he pried open the lemon to taste it.

"The islanders don't like us; they tolerate us in the name of commerce. If she liked you, she would have thrown you an apple." Kael chuckled as the crewmates began laughing.

The Ancient Map

On board the *Gilded Star*, the ancient map lay unfurled on a rough-hewn table bolted to the floor of the ship's cramped cabin, its parchment worn to threads at the folds. A goblet, a scatter of loose coins, and a candle pinned the corners. In the lamplight, fresh marks crowded the margins—circles and arrows, measurements and notes scratched tight, the desperate work of those who refused to leave fortune to chance. Jonas and Sabina hovered over the map, their voices held to a whisper as if the walls themselves might carry sound into the corridor. Her finger drew along three ridges and a winding river. His thumb pressed a crease flat as though he could smooth the centuries inside the folds.

"What makes you think it's authentic?" Sabina chided. "Some gypsy slips this into your pocket and sends us down a canyon to get robbed?"

Jonas scrutinized the map, noting its extreme age and the old language used in the markings.

"I've seen the other maps people use, and none of them have these landmarks or calculations," he replied.

"And why give it to you? Do you know her? Does she expect something in return?" Sabina said while pacing.

"Relax. I've never seen her before, and no, I don't know her. She just said something about a burden to bear, and then she was gone," Jonas said calmly.

Sabina realized he was being honest and tried to calm her overly suspicious nature. She moved beside him and studied the map's frail composition. "What if this is the map, and she couldn't bear keeping it any longer?" Sabina reasoned.

"Our map now," Jonas replied, making Sabina smile with confidence.

Sabina stepped out of the cabin and directed the crew to finish taking on provisions quickly.

Across the island ravines, engines rattled. Mechanics cursed and leaned into the heat of open hatches, coaxing failing pistons to hold steady as pilots sought the only kind of landing the Crescents allowed: careful, reluctant, exact. One wrong tilt of the nose and a hull would scrape stone; canvas would tear, and the voyage would end in ruin. Shipmates extended long poles outward to push away from any dangerous edge, in a concert of shouts and grunts until the tethers snapped tight as the ships touched down. Camps flared to life at the mouths of ravines—firelight flickering against rock, stacks of empty crates waiting like unpaid debts coming due.

Crews bathed in the river and walked paths to nearby taverns in search of the first mead permitted after weeks above the earth. Alcohol was forbidden on all ships, and with good reason. The tendency for quarrels and arguments had no place in a vessel where everyone had to trust each other while respecting the captain's orders. But once on land, mischief and bravado grew like wild vines clinging to the canyon walls. Trust was thin here. Treasure turned men into mirrors; most did not like what they saw.

Into the Temple

As the last light faded into night, the *Gilded Star* hovered above a remote canyon farther north than the camps where the fleet had landed. Jonas barked out orders as Sabina pointed to the landmarks on the map—matching them to local features. Sabina ran her fingertips across the paper as if feeling for a pulse. Ridgelines on parchment met ridgelines in stone below; river bends in ink met river bends in fog. She pointed into the mist.

"There," she said. "There—the mouth."

Jonas lifted his hand, and the crew moved at his signal. Ropes spun, engines sighed, and the ship descended carefully into a narrow cut, the canyon walls rising on either side like a throat swallowing whole. A mist rose up around the ship, blurring vision and confidence until a dull thud echoed in the canyon as they set down at last.

The crew had figured out their unique setting was not random and rushed to prepare. Without food or rest, they went in with pickaxes and rope, with sledgehammers and pry bars, with knives and a prayer here and there—mostly from men who hadn't prayed since childhood. The tunnels were carved by lava, with rounded walls, glass-smooth in places, sharp and treacherous in others. Heat pressed from below and around, a slow, steady exhale. Hours blurred into days. Runnels of sweat ran down backs and stung eyes. Darkness bit at the edges of the torches as if it were hungry too.

Then from the far-left passage came a sound—not wind, not voice, but the continuous roar of water buried in stone. They followed it and found an entrance where a carved mouth poured a shaft of falling water: the entrance to the temple. Torches burned within, though no hand was there to tend them, inviting them to enter.

Each man drank his fill of water, exhausted by the baking heat of lava flows moving through the walls. Jonas filled his canteen and handed it to Sabina.

"We're close, but the map only shows the entrance. We're on our own inside this maze," Sabina said.

The first chamber unfurled like a hall for some forgotten rite. The walls were carved with sigils of fire and sun, their gold inlay catching torchlight like eyes that watched from every angle. Sulfur drifted in faint flakes, falling like ash, as if the mountain itself were breathing.

Sabina held a torch and walked ahead, her excitement and lust for gold fueling her eager pace as she followed the path, turned a corner, and saw the main chamber.

"Gold!" she shrieked so loudly it echoed through the tunnels, making the men startle as they arrived behind her.

At the chamber's heart, piles of treasure lay in ceremonial rings—coins, plates, armlets—all encircling a pool of molten rock and black water. The pool shifted and coiled, moving like a serpent before the strike. The hoard of gold was not hidden. It was prepared, like an offering.

Crates slid across the floor. Hands wrapped in cloth went in and came out heavy; the gold was hot, searing skin if not protected. Sweat, soot, and a murmur that hovered between prayer and inventory filled the room. Each man kept a private pocket, because that was the agreement the captain pretended not to see: all take what they can bear, and the crew's portion split upon return.

Sabina stood beside her husband as he poured water from his canteen over an elaborate necklace with a large sapphire pendant. The metal cooled as Jonas gently wrapped the necklace around her neck.

"The last time this was worn, it was probably by an empress or queen," he whispered.

At last, the final crate tipped closed as the crew dragged the cargo through the tunnels on trolleys meant for mining. Jonas stood with Sabina in the empty chamber. She touched the pendant at her throat, shaking with excitement. He held a golden scepter in his hand, waving it like a king declaring a law.

"So much for curses," he said with a condescending laugh.

From a jagged niche inside the chamber, where torchlight did not reach, eyes watched them go. They were patient eyes. They had watched this scene before—the confident arrogance of possession in the hands of thieves.

Mercy's Poison

Mahala stepped into the emptied chamber once the echoes thinned to nothing. The light found no scar on her face, no crease at her mouth. Beauty draped her ageless body like a garment, unchanged by time. It had not always been so. She had once been a farmer's daughter, like the girls who now watched zeppelins pass. The great volcano came on a summer afternoon and rained fire through their valley. Flame took the house and bit at her until she could no longer see herself without flinching. Her body was mutilated, scars from head to toe, like a claw had raked across her, leaving her charred and broken in pain.

Her twin sister, Malina, carried her from the flames, saving her life but prolonging her suffering. Mahala wanted death—an end to the devastation of the volcano's wrath. But Malina never left her side, nursing Mahala back slowly, to stand, walk, and live. Malina said all the right gentle things; she even refused men's attention in favor of caring for her sister. But Mahala's eyes filled with envy. In each glance at her sister, she saw what she used to be and resented the presence of the untouched beauty Malina had.

In pain and fury, she prayed not only for healing but to outshine the sister whose pity cut deeper than the burn. Give me beauty again, she whispered to whatever would listen, and let my beauty cast a dark shadow on her. Give her my scars, my pain, so I can be the hero consoling her.

The darkness answered, but magic bound by blood is never precise. Mahala woke restored. Malina woke changed. Eternal youth had touched them both.

Malina did not understand the miraculous recovery her sister had made until jealousy rotted what the fire had spared. Mahala began scheming to destroy her sister, studying witchcraft, curses, and forbidden ways of the ancients.

"Why should Malina, unscarred and soft-voiced, be spared the weight of time? Why should kindness be rewarded when pain had been my price?" Mahala asked the darkness.

The darkness responded, defining the cost of her youth and beauty: Mahala could not leave the island, and her protection of the temple gold was the price. If the gold was taken, her scars would return by the next moon, and her years lived would be restored.

Mahala's beauty had become her prison. Malina's grace became her torment. A century is a long time to hate, driving the sisters apart, leaving Mahala alone in her bitter prison—trapped on the island with only her gold and bitterness for three hundred years. Malina found refuge in the arms of an aeronaut who took her away to Airovale, never to return to the Crescents.

Mahala stood in the empty chamber, calculating her wrath on those who had taken her gold. She walked through the splinters and debris left by the crew and noticed the ancient map among the rubble. It was the only map ever made of the temple, and Malina had taken it when she fled the island centuries ago. Mahala knew it was her sister's attempt to end her curse of long life.

The sensation of revenge pleased her dark soul. She smiled and spoke to herself as if her sister were listening.

"Clever move, dear sister. Finally showing you're not as sweet as everyone thought. Now it's my turn."

Mahala's Wrath

Across the island, crews awoke to the thud and ping of axes and chisels cutting copper from the mines. A constant dust blew from the old lava tunnels as loads of ore were carried to the ships. Within three days, their hulls were full, and eagerness to return home drove the men to work faster.

Some ventured off in search of the temple when the work had stopped for the day, but most spent their time and pay at the tavern, where meals, mead, and companionship were the cost of a day's wages. Such was the economy of the Crescent Islands; the alternatives were minimal food from the ship and long nights on the canyon floor.

Kael and his captain played cards by a lantern on the ship's deck. Their ship was fully loaded and ready to depart in the morning. They both knew better than to wander into the taverns, where games of chance and easy women led to bad decisions.

"We added the last of the supplies this afternoon," Kael said, laying a card down on a barrel head.

"Good. We can go at first light. I just need to check the jail for anyone we might be leaving behind," the captain replied in jest.

As the new moon appeared dark in the sky, a countdown had begun between the ships heading home and Mahala's curse to bring them down.

Mahala had left the temple and walked for days until she reached the black sand at sunrise. The tide licked at her ankles, tasting her rage. She pulled a piece of driftwood from the beach and drew long ovals in the wet grit—the shapes of balloons and hulls, noses tilted into wind, ropes trailing. She cupped seawater in her hands and poured it over each drawing until the lines blurred and ran back toward the foam. Her voice rose in a tongue older than the stone under her feet. She blew her breath across the sand, bitter and sharp.

"Bring them down, Aelmir," she said. "Break them open, and let the sea return what is mine."

Thunder answered from far off, not in sudden cracks but in measured booms that felt like footsteps approaching. A line of cloud muscled itself up from the horizon, swallowing color as it came. Lightning flickered inside it in a wash of blue like the flash of a blade. Once—just once—the storm itself took on the shape of a face: a broad brow, a white beard, a mouth that looked very nearly pleased.

The Storm Gathers

By then, the fleet had cleared the canyons and was making its way out over open water, all noses pointed toward the run home. Boilers hissed and rattled; chains clanked; canvas bellied. Hulls groaned under the weight of new fortune. Captains barked hoarse, and the men at the shovels learned how long a minute could be when flames burned hot.

The crews looked back at the dark veil coming after them, sails and steam churning to escape—but they were not evading. They were being driven into the hand of the monster.

On the cliff farms, the girls finished their rows and stacked their baskets. One of them stood a moment longer, listening as the last of the airships raced by. The sound wasn't the sea or the wind; it was heavier, like someone tall walking toward you without haste. A darkness shadowed overhead, and she knew it was time to seek shelter.

At sea, the wind swung the first wall of rain like a curtain of rock. Canvas snapped. Lanterns guttered. Ropes went tight, grinding and popping in resistance. Lightning drew white scars across the sky and left the taste of metal in the mouth. A voice—an echo—rolled across the fleets like laughter you pretend you didn't hear.

"Hold her!" a captain shouted. "Hold!"

The order drowned in the next peal.

Some ships climbed and held; others dipped, their noses stubborn and slow. A few rose, faltered, rose again. Coal shoveled faster did not make weight lighter. The men at the vents swore they could feel the storm lean down and set its hand against the canvas.

On the beach, Mahala's eyes did not blink. She watched in twisted pleasure as the rain chopped into the fleet like a knife. Each flash of lightning carved her smile sharper, each thunderclap like applause for her devotion. She did not need to touch the gold to own it; the ocean tide would return each piece on the waves of future days, as it always had.

She raised her arms to the storm, her voice rasping against the wind:

"Fools. It is not the gold that is cursed—it is me!"

Behind her, deep in the island's throat, the temple burned its low, patient light.

Far out to sea, a single ship lagged the rest, its engines stuttering from the sting of lightning. Clouds swallowed it before it could reach the others. Winds hammered the hull, driving it toward the abyss where dark sky and churning waves blurred to one line. The storm bent low, listening, as if waiting for the instant when metal would break and sea would claim it.

It was the *Nereid*. Aden clung to the rigging as the vessel groaned under the storm's hand, its fate teetering between the sky and the sea—yet somehow still aloft.

The night opened its mouth—and kept coming.

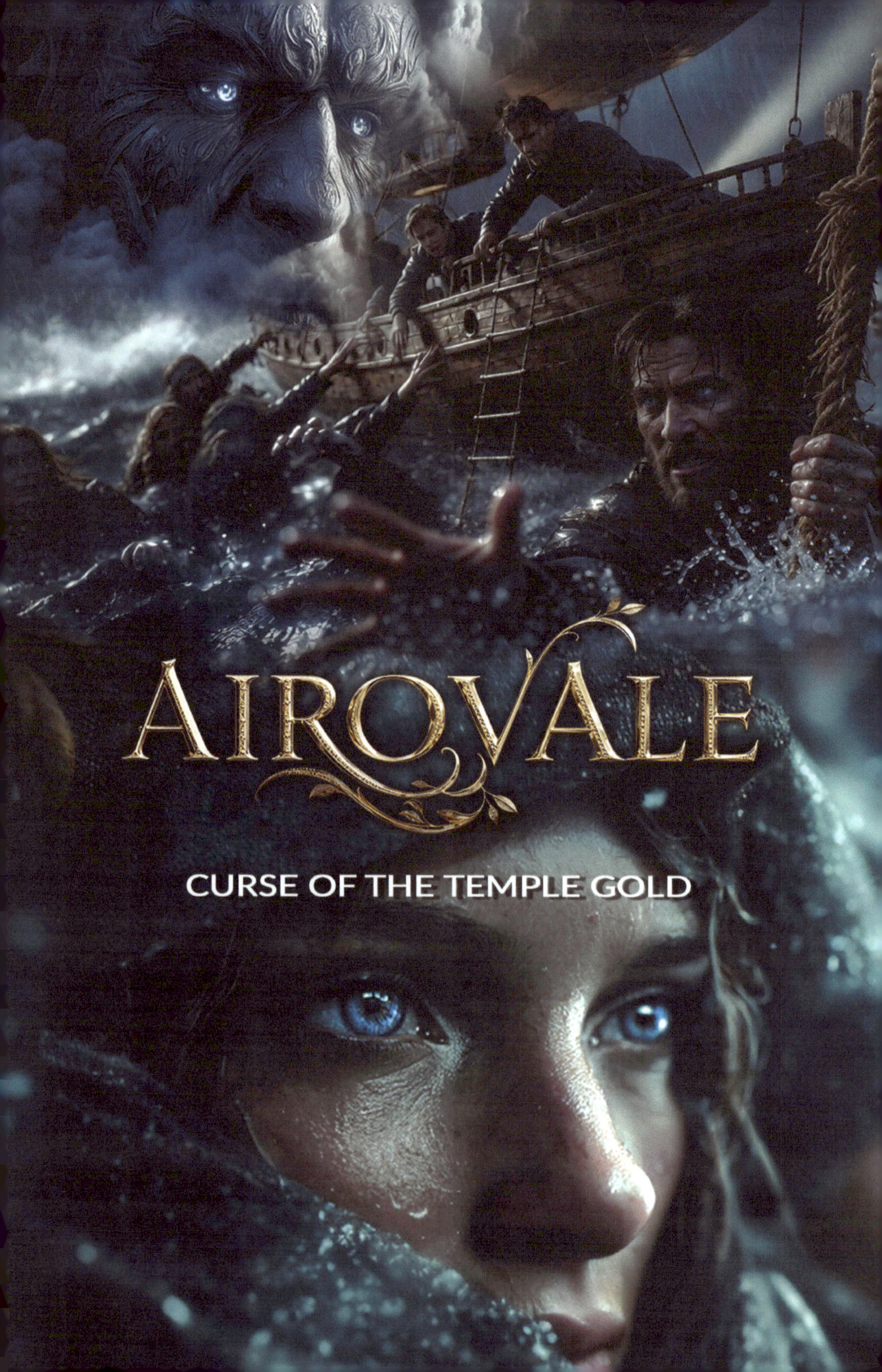

AIROVALE
CURSE OF THE TEMPLE GOLD

Curse of the Temple Gold

The Storm Circles

The storm circled at first, prowling the horizon in silence. Black clouds amassed, heavy and deliberate, blotting out the edge of the world. The fleet stretched wide across the open sea—freighters sagging with copper, traders creaking at their seams, lean vessels shivering against the wind. They were an uneven line, the singed air around them tense with the feeling of being watched. Every eye turned upward, outward, waiting.

Men checked instruments that had never failed them before. Gauges quivered where they should have held steady. A helmsman wiped his palms on his coat and laughed once, too loudly, as if to prove the sound of his own voice could still exist beneath the sky. Somewhere along the line, a captain ordered more steam, another ordered less, and the disagreement rippled outward—not in words, but in hesitation.

Aelmir's eyes opened.

The first crack split the sky as if it had broken apart. The sound echoed through bone and blood, a hammer blow that shook ribs and stole breath. Men flinched as though struck themselves, hands tightening on wheel and line. They looked to one another for assurance, afraid to show fear but overwhelmed as dread surged through their bodies. Rigging strained and creaked while pilots muttered broken oaths, clinging to their helms. Every instinct screamed to seek shelter, though none could be found in the open sky.

The thunder did not roll away. It lingered—pressed down, close enough to feel.

The next crack felt deliberate, as if an invisible force had stepped closer. Thunder smashed down like stone ground to dust, a reminder of how small they all were beneath it. Then a chaotic flash of blue lit the heavens, branching like veins across the living sky, until one jagged line pierced its prey.

Lightning speared one of the heavily loaded freighters, and her copper payload burst in a torrent of emerald flame. The vessel became a torch, so bright it washed across the sky and illuminated the fleet around it. For a heartbeat, even the storm seemed to pause, admiring its own lethality. Crews blinked against the glare, shadows sliding across their faces as wreckage fell like rain set on fire. The doomed freighter's nose split the waves in a plume of steam and smoke, swallowed by the churning darkness of the sea.

The scene burned itself into memory. Each blink revived the silhouette—a phantom ship aflame in green, haunting them long after it was gone. The storm remained, the aftertaste of lightning filled the air, and the knowledge settled over them all: one had been chosen. More would follow.

Lightning Strikes

Haunting shrieks from the storm clouds mixed with engines straining to gain another inch of height or speed, to outrun the judgment closing around them.

One ship arched high, just clearing a spear of lightning that would have split her in two. Another twisted away, but the wind followed like a predator closing in. Lightning tore across the fleet, talons of storm and fury ripping canvas and wood. Ropes snapped loose, men shouted, and the airships scattered—each vessel marked by dread, knowing the storm was still hunting.

A freighter lost control of her rudder, holding steady for a breath as her crew worked to repair it. Then she drifted into the grip of a dark cloud and burst into flames, raining fire on ships below as she floated on, unaware of her own doom.

A family's hot-air balloon hung near the rear of the fleet, its painted canopy already frayed by the journey across the magnetic sea. They had come to the Crescents for copper, not gold—an adventure meant to secure a future for their children. When the first bolt struck, the balloon leapt like a toy in a child's hand. Flame ran down its rigging, claws of fire raking the fabric.

Parents grabbed their children, shoving them over the basket's edge, screaming for them to jump.

The balloon rose as it burned, buoyed by heat even as it died.

One child slipped, hands clawing empty air as he fell into the sea below. Another clung to her mother's sleeve as she was pushed free, only for the woman to be swallowed by fire as the balloon tore itself apart.

Into the Sea

From the nearby deck of the *Ironwind*, the zeppelin's captain and crew watched the catastrophe unfold. He leaned over the port bow, horror carved into his face.

"Drop her lower!" he roared.

His first mate, Kael, repeated the command, voice booming above the storm. Lines flew. The *Ironwind* groaned as she sank dangerously close to the sea, spray slapping her hull. Ropes spilled over the rails, flailing downward like desperate arms reaching into the white caps below.

On the deck above, sailors fought with the winches, fingers numb, muscles screaming. The dinghy creaked downward, far too slow. Below, children and passengers flailed in the turbulent water, their cries thinning beneath the roar. Burning wreckage cast light across the waves, illuminating survivors while seeming to lure the *Ironwind* closer to peril.

Kael's eyes narrowed. He knew the sea would claim them long before the boat reached the surface.

He thought of Mira's voice—steady, warm. He thought of the promise he had made without knowing how it would be tested.

He seized a line, lashed it tight around his waist, tested the knot once—and leapt.

The fall punched the breath from his chest as the rope snapped taut, biting deep into his ribs. Then the sea swallowed him whole. Salt burned his throat. Cold cut like iron. Darkness snapped shut around him as he dangled beneath the waves. For a heartbeat he hung suspended in the silent deep, the storm above reduced to muffled thunder, until his lungs clawed for air and his body surged upward into spray and chaos.

The rope groaned under the strain as the crew hauled to keep him tethered, but Kael pushed forward, fighting waves that rose like walls. Firelight and darkness offered only flashes—cries half-heard, hands vanishing as quickly as they appeared in the lightning's strobe. Still, he drove himself on.

Children screamed. Tiny fingers slipped again and again in the slick water. He caught one boy by the collar, another girl by the wrist, pulling them close as waves crashed over his head. He shoved them toward the lowered dinghy, dragging breath in ragged bursts between strokes.

Above, his shipmates strained to keep him in sight, lanterns swinging wildly. The line jerked hard as the sea dragged him under, then slackened as he surfaced again, teeth clenched against the gale. He found two girls clinging to the balloon's shredded rigging, their knuckles white. He climbed onto the wreckage, pried their grip loose, and shoved them toward the *Ironwind's* ropes.

The Woman on the Wreckage

An oil slick ignited, flashing fire across the wreckage. The flames illuminated a woman farther out than he had expected to search. She clung to the mast of her shattered craft, lips moving in soundless prayer, eyes empty and unfocused.

Kael swam to her and threw a rope. She did not reach for it.

She stared into the chaos as if holding the mast alone could keep her alive.

Kael climbed onto the wreckage and fought the swell to reach her. The *Ironwind* shifted sideways, drifting close enough for a lifeline from the deck. Men shouted for speed. Kael felt his own mind grow strangely calm as he understood the truth—this woman was not fully present. Her eyes looked past him. Through him. She clung to the mast but saw nothing.

He tied the lifeline around them both, then knelt and took her face in his hands.

"This is no longer your ship," he said, voice raw, eyes steady. "Let the sea have it. Come with me."

He pried her fingers loose as she closed her eyes and surrendered. Kael gathered her against him and nodded to the crew. They hauled them up just as the wreckage rolled and vanished beneath the waves.

Kael handed her off and turned back toward the water, already moving—

A hand caught his shoulder.

"Hold on, first mate," the captain barked.

"There are no more splashes," he said grimly. "No hands in view. The sea has taken the rest. And I need you here, you bloody lunatic."

He wrapped a blanket around Kael and steered him back aboard.

"Are they caring for the survivors?" Kael asked hoarsely.

The captain nodded. "They are. But we have a bigger problem."

Sacrifice

The *Ironwind* listed forward, her nose dipping into the waves, cold spray washing the deck.

"Too many aboard. We're overloaded. She won't rise."

The captain stared at the shivering survivors, then at the chests stacked along the rails. Copper. Tons of it. His jaw hardened.

"Over the side!" he shouted, ripping open the nearest chest.

Kael joined him, soaked and shivering, as they heaved copper into the sea until the crate was light enough to throw overboard. Nuggets vanished without sound, like coins dropped into a bottomless well.

A crew member's voice cracked as he shouted over the roar of the wind. "Certainly not all sir? Just enough to get us aloft?"

The men began to slowly dump the copper, delaying their full compliance in hopes to not sacrifice everything.

"Open your greedy eyes, we're taking on water by the ton! This monster is eating us alive," the captain barked.

"You heard him!" Kael shouted. "Dump the load or we all go under tonight!"

For a heartbeat the crew froze. The voyage. The cost. The promise. All of it lay in those crates.

A heavy wave smashed the bow, water pouring across the deck. The hesitation broke. Men heaved chests overboard, one after another. The sound became a rhythm—a booming splash, a ritual sacrifice. Slowly, painfully, the *Ironwind* rose.

Kael staggered forward, shaking violently. His eyes found the last crate.

"Do we keep it?" he asked.

The captain shook his head. "Give it to them. They lost everything. We're only wet."

The Gilded Star

As the *Ironwind* climbed clear of the storm, lightning reflected off the hull of the *Gilded Star*, still trapped in Aelmir's chaos. She sagged lower, the weight of temple gold grinding against her struts. Rain hammered the deck as crewmen flung coins and armlets into the sea.

"It will pull you under the moment you touch the water," Jonas shouted. "We'll all sink if we don't jettison the gold!"

Sabina clutched a crate, eyes fever-bright. "Maybe they can swim to shore," she hissed. "Why should we lose everything for them?"

The men turned on her.

"Lady," one growled, "if you want the treasure, you can swim with it."

They tore open crates and hurled gold into the storm. Sabina screamed, clawing at them, but Jonas dragged her into the cabin, holding her as her fists pounded his chest.

Once inside, he held her hands and pushed her into a chair to keep her from going back on deck.

"Sabina!" he shouted, his harsh tone stunned her movements. "This won't bring him back!"

Jonas looked in her eyes, watching his guarded words sink in.

"I know," Sabina calmed as her body began to collapse in his arms. "I just wanted to think about something other than…"

"Letting go?" Jonas sighed.

"The despair, it consumes me like this storm, chewing away everything until nothing is left."

The ship rocked sideways as the winds outside bashed against the hull. The voices of the crew mixed with splintered thuds of crates being tossed overboard.

Jonas held on to a post, steadying them both against a bulkhead. "It's just gold, what future can it give if we're unable to live it?"

They paused in silence, as their breathing calmed.

"We found the treasure though," Sabina whispered. "Nothing to show for it, but no one can take that from us."

The *Gilded Star* had risen above the storm line into calmer winds. The crew went below to get warm in the boiler room.

"Surviving would be something and trying again even more." Jonas sighed as he stood and guided her to her feet.

"Oh, I'm done with chasing treasure." she chuckled while wiping the tears from her face.

Jonas smiled, watching his wife's face return from when they first fell in love, "I wasn't talking about treasure."

Dawn

By dawn the sea was littered with canvas and splintered wood. Half the fleet was gone. The rest limped home, smoking and scarred.

On the *Ironwind's* deck, a young woman with deep blue eyes sat among the survivors. Wrapped in a blanket, she watched her breath cloud and vanish. Her life lay in pieces behind her, scattered across the sea.

She drew the blanket tighter. She felt richer than any queen.

She was alive.

AIROVALE
COMING HOME

Coming Home

The Tower Bells

Morning in Airovale was painted over the Southern Sea in pale strokes of gold. From the horizon beyond, the first zeppelins dotted the sky just above the waterline. The watchman in the bell tower yawned as he stretched back in his chair, rubbing his eyes from a long shift. He stood and rolled the stiffness caused by the night air from his shoulders as his eyes scanned the ever-empty horizon that hadn't changed in days. The dots caught his focus. He squinted, waiting to dismiss them as birds or debris in his eyelashes. The only ships that would arrive from the north would be those inbound from the Crescent Islands—it was the fleet!

"Fleet arriving, north port!" he shouted in a crackled voice, reaching for the rope that rang the tower bells.

His voice echoed over the silent village, followed by the ceremonial clang of bells reserved for ships that made Airovale their home port. It was more than the daily routine of ship movements in the capital city; it was a homecoming that honored aeronauts as heroes of the village.

Upon hearing the tower bells, each family member of an aeronaut would don goggles in solidarity. Within minutes, spouses, children, and parents began emerging from their homes en route to the docks and airfields to greet their loved ones. The village custom was deeply respected, and if you saw your loved one aboard their ship before docking, it was considered a sign of devotion and good luck.

The aeronauts also stood shoulder to shoulder along the edges of their ships, to see and be seen, waving to their families below. If the mission was for agriculture, a portion of the fruits would be tossed to the crowd. Mercantile voyages were celebrated with flowers thrown to women and girls, while mining missions consisted of tossing small coins or nuggets from the mines.

As the bells rang from the tower, their iron chimes called people to wake and prepare for the ceremony. Word spread quickly: the fleet had returned. The streets flushed with crowds on their way to the designated moorings for each zeppelin.

Wives and young ladies helped each other braid hair, adjusting corsets and minding children who ran in all directions. The anticipation of reunion was contagious—joyful and filled with speculation. What stories would the men share as they unloaded copper by the ton, or maybe gold in secret?

Irina stepped onto her veranda as the bells chimed in the distance, her home positioned over the northern bay where the ships slowly approached. She held her newborn son in her arms, sighing in relief that the journey was complete and her husband had returned. She had suffered many dreams of dread while he was away and feared a horrible fate awaited him. When he left, she had not yet delivered, making her even more anxious and excited to be reunited with him.

She looked quickly to identify his ship, but they were eclipsed in the sunrise and still too far away. She began walking toward the field where his ship docked, away from the port, where the winds were more favorable.

Broken Fleet

The port and aerial fields filled quickly with eager families, pointing and speculating, struggling to identify names in the bright morning sun. As the ships drew closer, the truth became apparent as the crowds reacted in unison, remarking on the condition of the vessels.

Canvases were torn and scorched; engines smoked and groaned as if each breath might be the last, barely making enough fire to hold a hover or steam to push forward.

Crews stood shoulders apart, their faces muddied with soot and salt. Some were bandaged, others propped up by crutches or by each other. The storm had broken them, but left them alive to tell the tale.

Crowds began murmuring, guessing, as the elders who no longer flew began to admit what they recognized. The gifts would be different today—but more precious.

"Where are the other ships?" a woman in the crowd protested, not realizing what others already understood.

The Count

From her tower, Elara leaned out her window, knowing immediately the count was much lower than expected. She strained to read the names of the airships with a telescope, calling them out to Garrick as he checked them off in her log. Each ship name found on the list was a victory.

"I think it's the *Ironwind*... she's really beat up," Elara shouted while searching for more ships.

"Got it!" Garrick confirmed, checking the name with relief.

"Oh! *Gilded Star*!" Elara said excitedly as the light flashed off her telescope. "And *Leviathan*, and *Behemoth*!"

These were more than ship names to them both; these were friends, colleagues, generations of lives interwoven in their world.

Elara stayed at her window, hoping more ships might appear, while Garrick counted the sum quietly. He already recognized the signs of a failed journey, and the Crescent Islands were known for their cruel storms.

Elara collapsed her telescope and set it on her desk, walking toward Garrick to look at the ledger.

Garrick hesitated, holding it to himself as the reality set in.

"Dad, how many?" Elara insisted.

"Two turned back, leaving ten," he said, pretending to count but purposely delaying the answer.

"How many are still out there?!" Elara said, snatching the ledger from his hands.

"None," Garrick replied as he walked to the window and looked out at the horizon. "Five came home. The rest..." Garrick paused. "Not even the *Nereid*, my old ship."

Elara closed her ledger and sat on the floor, sobbing, overcome with the impact of so many lost.

"They could still be out there—we don't know!" she said, tears streaming down her face.

"Aye, we'll keep looking," Garrick said, pulling her to her feet and placing the telescope into her hand. "That's what we do."

Salvaged Souls

A long shadow passed over the tower as the *Ironwind* moved inland. The caked salt spray on the hull began to flake away as the warmer air brushed across the canvas. Kael and the captain stood along the deck rail with the crew, survivors filled in between them. They headed for the airfield, knowing it would take time to match survivors with families spread across the village.

Mira's auburn hair blew in the breeze as she hurried through the lane, eyes wide as she recognized the markings on Kael's airship. Her smile outpaced her steps as she tried to keep up with it, noting the damage and crowded deck line.

She passed a child perched in her grandfather's arms, pointing her tiny hand at the *Ironwind*. "That one!" she cried, goggles slipping down her brow to match her father's.

The old man's lined face broke into a rare smile, relief seeping into his bones as he recognized his son's ship among the survivors.

"Yes, very good! Let's go see Daddy!" the elderly man said as he followed behind Mira's path to the field.

News spread quickly of the storm's terror and the grim reality of mortal loss. Each vessel on the horizon was hope that fate had spared the daring family members who ventured to the Crescents in search of fortune.

Across the ports, an older man looked down from the *Behemoth*—a tiny ship—and caught sight of a silver-haired woman waving from the crowd. His wife. His home. He tugged at the rigging to lower the ship as his fear of never seeing her again melted away. The distance between them closed in heartbeats, though they had lived this reunion dozens of times before. Each voyage was a gamble; each embrace a reprieve. And this, he swore, would be his last.

Then the *Ironwind* descended, her hull scarred by flame and sea. Salt mixed with oil crusted along her flanks, bearing silent testimony to the storm's fury. From her deck, Kael stepped down the plank, Mira rushing to meet him. She searched his face and knew tragedy had passed upon him—too many missing ships where once there had been many.

His words came heavy with regret. "So many... lost."

But she pressed her hands to his cheeks, tears and gratitude spilling together. "You came back to me," she whispered. "You're my treasure."

The *Ironwind's* captain passed the remaining copper to each of the survivors, bidding them luck as they went to rebuild their lives. The captain and Kael locked eyes and nodded. They understood the real treasure was each soul saved.

A village messenger arrived by horse and rushed to the *Ironwind's* captain.

"Is it true? You took on survivors?" he asked urgently.

"Yes—not all, but we took as many as we could save," the captain replied. "Please tell the others. These people need some hope."

The messenger nodded and quickly mounted his horse, heading toward the docks where crowds stood in desperation, hoping the news of survivors might change their grief.

Kael and Mira embraced as she checked his wounds and fussed over each scratch. One by one, strangers approached them, thanking Kael for saving them. He was humbled by their gratitude, and in that moment Mira understood he had done more than survive—he had been their savior.

"Where will they go?" Mira asked as two young sisters, still wrapped in blankets, walked aimlessly from the ship. They looked into Kael's eyes with the same fear he had seen when pulling them from the water. They could not answer, knowing their only family had perished in the storm.

Kael and Mira looked at each other without hesitation—no discussion, only the purity of empathy and mutual love that could sustain all.

Mira gently offered her hand to the girls, "You can come with home us."

Kael smiled, reaching down to lift the smaller girl in his arms, grunting as his bruises pinched. Their bond formed in that moment, walking home together, learning each other's names, as a family from that day forward.

In the port, Alina carried her small daughter to the docks. The ship she waited for never appeared. The cruel realization that his ship had gone down moved over her like ice-cold water as she held her baby close, tears flowing while watching other families reunite.

The village messenger arrived, shouting news of possible survivors as the crowds quickly moved toward the airfield. Grief was still new; each hoped they would not have to bury their beloved that day. As long as a chance of survival existed, their aeronauts were still alive.

Alina followed the crowd, slowly at first, then gently pushing through in anticipation. She arrived at the *Ironwind,* her eyes scanning the mass of wandering people—confusion, shouting, joy all mixed together. She told herself to stay in one place and slowly turn, checking every face, but her eyes blurred as tears streamed down her cheeks.

"Papa," her daughter said unexpectedly.

"What?" Alina asked in disbelief. Her daughter only knew a few words, but she spoke confidently.

"What? Where's Papa?" Alina prompted.

Her daughter pointed toward the *Ironwind*, where a man on crutches was being guided down the gangplank. He was heavily bandaged and moved very slowly due to his injuries.

"Oh, thank God!" Alina gasped as she rushed to his side.

Alina held her daughter in one hand as her husband put his arm over her shoulder. They moved slowly, awkwardly, toward the village.

A horse-drawn cart slowed and stopped beside them. It was Kateryna's family, bringing hay from the field. Her father handed the reins to Kateryna as he stepped down to help Alina and her husband climb into the back with their baby.

"Thank you so much!" they said in unison.

"We are all going the same way, no?" Kateryna's father replied in a warm foreign accent.

The cart continued as those words settled in their minds. He was not talking about a trip through the village; it was more than that.

Late Arrival

Farther down the field, two smaller ships had departed for their home destinations. Traders, separated from the returning fleet, gave momentary distraction as they appeared in the sky, pushing into the wind toward the eastern islands. Then the horizon returned to an empty graveyard of lost hope.

Irina had arrived at the mooring for her husband Doran's ship. Others stood nearby—families of the crew—all hoping for a late arrival after walking past mourners along the docks and fields.

She had watched him ascend just five weeks ago, her feet in the same clump of tall grass, a baby still inside her. It felt like another lifetime. Becoming a mother had given her new eyes, a new focus on what mattered. She had begged him to bring back a refined dress, jewelry, her heart set on extravagance. Now her only longing was a father for her child, a home, a life shaped and devoted to family.

How quickly the sparkle of material distractions had faded, and the maturity of a woman had emerged. She looked at her son, sleeping in her arms, and took a deep breath, hoping she would not be raising him alone.

"I see her!" a voice erupted in the crowd. "She's smoking like wet leaves on fire, but there she is!"

A small vessel, tattered with rips and patched by the crew's clothing, drifted into view. A plume of soot poured from the failing engine as she slid into the grass without a sound.

Irina could see Doran's bright smile already as he leaped from the ship and ran to her.

Without a word, she placed her baby in Doran's arms and watched his reaction with joy. She was not the woman he had left behind; she saw herself and him completely different now. She felt the strength of his presence, like a shield that comforted beyond words. They were a family that had been given a chance to survive. As her heart filled with emotions, her playful character emerged.

"You're late," she teased, as they often did.

"Yeah, had to stop and do the laundry," he replied, never taking his eyes off hers. "Been busy?" He motioned as he looked again at his newborn son, overwhelmed by every detail.

"Little bit. Hungry?" she said, pulling him with her.

Irina walked with Doran and their son through the streets, grateful he had survived, grateful not to be one of the women drowning in tears on every corner. They arrived home, and she left the baby in his arms as she prepared a welcoming meal. Doran waited for the taste of home while looking into his son's eyes, astonished by every detail.

"He looks like me!" Doran said proudly as tiny fingers curled around his thumb.

"Yeah, sorry about that," Irina replied while taking a pan from the stove.

Wonder and humility welled in him, greater than any treasure promised across the sea. He had almost lost everything and could not stop marveling at how close he had come to the edge of oblivion.

Irina set a plate of food in front of him and sat beside him. Doran held their son and began devouring the meal she had made. He hadn't eaten in days, but his thoughts were on his newborn son and being with his wife.

"So, I've been thinking about this career of yours," she began while putting more food on his plate.

"We're going to be farmers now," he said abruptly, pausing as he pulled a heavy bag of copper coins from his belt—setting it on the table.

Irina's eyes grew wide in surprise. She had expected him to resist her idea, but instead he was already in agreement, thinking ahead of her about what to do and how.

She paused while watching him continue eating, delighted, shocked, and melting into his strength. He was her man, her fortress, and she had almost lost him.

"Is that… treasure?" she asked playfully.

"No—this is," he replied, holding his son closer. "You are."

"Good answer," she giggled, dropping their familiar banter and embracing him tightly, knowing every moment forward was a gift. She became soft, unable to express her thoughts, and set their baby in his basket to sleep.

Vigil

Not all found happiness that day. Some waited on the docks until sunset, scanning the horizon, asking the surviving ships for information, describing their lost ones to anyone who would listen. Their loved ones had been taken, and the sea did not give back. An eerie wailing rose through the village, cries of sorrow moving through the air. Aeronauts kept silent—grateful to be spared, consumed by guilt for surviving. Candles burned in windows across the city, honoring the lost.

Elara tearfully looked out at the half-moon casting light on the dark horizon. The scent of cloves filled the air from the smoke curling out of Garrick's pipe. He sat by the window, watching it all. He had seen this before. Ships leave. Ships return. Fortunes are gained; lives are lost. He drew deeply, exhaled slowly, and let the smoke drift like a ghost of all who had gone, out the window and into the sky.

His thoughts moved through memories like hallways in his mind—faces, voices, moments shared. He tried to put words to it all, to make sense of the senseless, as the old parable returned in his mind:

Time is the only treasure; spent by the choices we make.

The aeronauts had left in pursuit of wealth and returned with hands almost empty, yet only now could they see how rich they had been all along. We leave what we have to chase desire, then surrender the gain in exchange for what was already ours. In the end, it is not gifts or fame, but the faces at the docks, the hands waving from below, reminding us that the only treasure worth chasing is coming home.

AIROVALE
CANYON MYST

Canyon Myst

The Storm

They had set their course for the Crescent Islands, a remote outpost rich in copper and legendary gold. But time and chance were crafting a storm—whispered as an ancient curse, sealed in a land no map dared name.

The tempest struck the *Nereid* without mercy. The wind ripped through rigging, fire tore across fuel lines, engines sputtered and died in choking fumes. The proud vessel spun helpless, a gilded crown of propellers slowing into silence.

She should have broken in half, but her design was rigid and true, tested through decades of storms. Instead, she was hurled forward at a speed no aeronaut had ever known. The wind sheared planks from her hull like shavings beneath a carpenter's block, stripping her down to a patchwork of exposed boards and interior fittings.

Then the clouds closed in.

Adrift

For weeks the ship drifted above the earth, off course in punitive exile by a storm only legend could explain. The *Nereid* had vanished from existence, adrift like a ghost swallowed by endless vapors. No compass held true, no map bore their place. Only sky and sea, cruel and endless. The crew moved like shades within the gondola. Hunger gnawed at them, candles guttered to stubs beside charts that no longer mattered. Their vessel limped onward into the forgotten blue of the Southern Sea—beyond reach, beyond hope.

Distant clouds taunted them with shapes of mountains, but no birds to give hope, no fish below, only emptiness disguised as the open sea.

Some whispered they had already died. That this was their torment, to sail forever without landfall, entombed aloft.

Rain would come, offering a chance to gutter water into barrels—salvation from thirst disguised as blessing, while survival itself extended their torment. The crew gathered around the barrel each day as water was rationed with near-religious care. When the supply ran low, barely a taste was given.

In the early morning, cloud cover above and below cast the ship into a dark void. Movement felt suspended, as if the *Nereid* hovered in place, with only the rattling of torn rigging and loose canvas to signal a breeze. Just before sunrise, each man was given a half cup from the rain barrel.

"I remember the times I left a drink half full on the table and walked away," a crewman said, swallowing his portion for the day.

"Where are we, Captain?" Aden asked in a dry voice, staring up at the blank sky above them. It was his first time over the open sea.

"There's no map to mark the way when the stars disappear," Von Holt replied. The experienced aeronauts nodded in agreement, knowing better than to ask what was already understood.

Aden had known hunger before, but he had never known the brutality of thirst. His face and lips blistered beneath the sun, his body stiff with fatigue, salt marbled his clothing. He cut a strip of leather from his boot and kept it between his teeth, a trick learned on the streets of Airovale—to dull the ache of hunger and distract the mind.

Hours later, a seagull fluttered and landed on the deck rail. It observed the crew, surveying in each direction as they languished along the edges of the gondola —skin cracked, eyes sunken, breath shallow. Within a moment it raised its wings and lifted into the wind.

No one moved, but all noticed. They questioned their own minds if that had just happened, or was the delirium getting worse?

One by one, the men struggled to their feet, hands gripping the railing as bodies protested the effort. They leaned out over the edge of the gondola, scanning the horizon with eyes that had nearly forgotten how to look for anything but sky.

In the distance, an island, due east, backlit by the rising sun. The clouds had spread apart, exposing it like a jewel of hope, set on sparkling water.

"Land!" a crewmen said in a whisper, afraid he was wrong.

Then others began to repeat that single word, murmuring became convincing as their voices grew in excitement. A speck on the horizon, solitary and still. It could have been a scrap of mercy or another mirage of their purgatory, but the wind was pushing them toward it.

Landfall

Aden was sent to burn the last nuggets of coal in the hold, giving the vessel limited navigation as they attempted a landing. Smoke billowed from the cracked furnace, spewing ash and fumes into the tailwind as it curled back across the deck.

The captain knew there was only one chance, one pass at landing. Lowering altitude meant no way to rise again, and to blow by the field would be the end of all hope. He lined up his sights with the volcanic mound on the island and steered them down into a clearing hemmed by towering trees, engines coughing their last. Canvas scraped branches, timbers groaned, the ground rose to meet them. It was not a landing but a fall with grace enough to leave them breathing. They stumbled out into the hush of green, weak and desperate, alive only because the island had allowed it.

The feel of land beneath their feet was haunting, heavy, undeserved. They had seen entire ships consumed in bolts of fury across the open sea, and yet here they stood. A second chance had been given.

The captain, pragmatic and strong, remembered his role. They were no longer adrift as equals; they were once again a crew with a mission. Their first priority: food.

"We'll keep to the ship for shelter, tether her down tight, and spread out. See what we can eat and carry jugs for water wherever you find it." Von Holt ordered.

At the end of their first day, they sat around a campfire, eating for the first time in weeks. Hunger drove them to devour every morsel, hands shaking with anticipation and weakness.

"Do you think we can repair the ship?" an aeronaut asked the captain.

"We'll try," Von Holt said, chewing through a skewer of lizard. "But we'll need parts. And coal. A great deal of it."

A crewman suddenly stood, staggered, and turned away from the fire, vomiting into the undergrowth.

The men laughed and cheered, knowing he had eaten too quickly after their lengthy ordeal.

"Slow down, you idiot!" Von Holt jabbed. "Your body has forgotten what food is."

The men sipped at their water jugs, hoping to avoid the same outcome.

As the crewman cleared his throat away from the fire, he looked up and saw a thin pillar of smoke rising in the far distance.

He turned back and asked, "Is that from the volcano?"

Silence fell over the men, as the first mate stood and shielded his eyes from the campfire.

"What do you think, Steffan? Maybe an open vent from the mountain?" Von Holt questioned.

Steffan was the captain's first mate, and had the best vision of the crew.

"It's not some random lava flow—the flash pattern is more like...that." Steffan said, turning to point at their fire.

"Well then, let's hope they are friendly," Von Holt sighed while pounding his chest from indigestion.

In the morning the captain sent a team of aeronauts and crew to investigate the distant smoke. He instructed them to keep their knives concealed when encountered, and to investigate their resources for possible parts.

"If we are stuck here, it's better to begin with peaceful gestures. But, if you're not back in 3 days, we're coming after you." Von Holt said, as he sent Steffan and the team into the jungle.

Into the Jungle

Dressed for altitude, they sweated in their heavy leathers, trudging through vines and mist. Knives were useful in cutting a path through the dense vegetation, but movements were slow and labored in the heat. Around them, unseen, golden fireflies hovered like patient eyes—the invisible fae watching, guarding, waiting.

The forest swallowed them quickly. Shafts of sunlight pierced the canopy in narrow columns, painting the ground in shifting mosaics. The air was thick, damp, alive with the cries of unseen birds and the rattle of insects. Once, the earth trembled faintly beneath their boots—something large moving far below, too deep to glimpse, but near enough to remind them they were trespassers in this strange world.

It was nothing like the maps of explorers, nothing like the harsh frontiers they had known. Rocks seemed twice as large, vines grew thick and endless, even the currents in the streams pulled at them as they waded across. Was it a land of giants, or had hunger and exhaustion driven them past their senses?

Nothing was larger than it should have been. It only felt that way, as though the island itself leaned inward, compressing their sense of scale.

They went a full day's walk, grueling and harsh. Tiny glowing insects, hovered above the ferns, and moss-covered rocks, marking a natural trail that led them through the jungle. One of the crew tried to catch one in his hand but it always evaded his grasp.

"Maybe, I could make a lure out of them to catch fish," said the crewman as his distracted steps slowed the team down.

"And maybe they're poisonous?" Steffan snapped, his annoyance speaking for the team.

The men grunted in agreement, and continued on their mission.

By sunset they reached the final climb toward the village in the distance. This was it—the source of the smoke, the sound of voices echoing into the valley below. Their excitement built, paranoia mingled with hope. They kept their hands on their weapons, out of sight but ready.

As they climbed, Steffan saw what looked like a child's face hidden in the trees. It was watching them, then turned and vanished when he made eye contact. He paused while holding on to the vines, catching his breath. He tipped his canteen for the last drops of water he had, while surveying out over the island. From his vantage point, he could retrace their path, and see the smoke from the *Nereid* crash site.

In the valley beneath them, the roar of a large panther rattled in the brush, as small birds emerged in scattered flight.

The men hesitated, looking at each other in doubt. Unsure if they should climb faster or hide. They felt surrounded, vulnerable, and exhausted as they made their way up the vine-covered hill.

"Whatever that is, it knows we're here." Steffan said quietly, hoping to keep the men calm.

Step by step they mounted the last hill, catching the scent of food in the breeze, a joyful tune, a rushing waterfall. Had they survived—or was this how death welcomed the frail and broken?

Canyon Myst

They stumbled into the village drenched in sweat, their black coats hanging like shrouds. Walking in a trance, gazing at a village carved into canyon walls. Wooden decks stretched over tranquil rivers, markets laden with gleaming fruits, taverns pouring ale, musicians in full song, cobblers, tailors, blacksmiths at their forges, and the scent of meat roasting in the air.

Suddenly the music stopped, and the crowds turned to see them standing in the street.

The smoke had been a beacon, an invitation to step into paradise—and as the crew stood in awe of their surroundings, the villagers began to approach. Barra, a broad-shouldered man with steel at both hip and shoulder pushed through the crowd, his presence cutting a path before him, determined to be the first to greet them.

"Welcome, gentlemen! Did your ship run aground on the rocks?" he asked.

He looked them over, one by one, grunting in disapproval.

"Uh... zeppelin, our engines were struck by—" one of the pilots replied.

"That would explain the long coats. You look thin and smell of sweat and coal, all of you," the man said with a booming voice. The crowd laughed and ogled them as they circled around.

"Bring food, and give them a wash in the river, urgently—and find something less... whatever this is," he said, pointing at their clothing.

The man's authority seemed to carry enormous weight, the people did not hesitate to respond to his instructions, as they began introducing themselves, guiding the crew toward the river that ran from a waterfall at the edge of the canyon. Each villager introduced themselves, as if there was nothing unusual about the crew's presence at all.

"Tell the tavern to put a round on my account," the burly man shouted as the villagers attended to each crew member as if they were royalty.

Barra was the village leader, forceful, quick-tempered, yet shrewd enough to guide the business of the people. Castaways were rare, and their sudden appearance always stirred a ripple of excitement through the canyon. Children whispered and pointed, merchants pressed forward with gifts, and neighbors craned for a closer look—as if strangers carried not only stories, but a rare echo of the outside world the canyon had faded from memory.

Barra established his dominance, and then withdrew, letting the villagers' warmth envelop the newcomers. The crew were in shock, overwhelmed by the kindness of the people. The villagers pressed food and drink into their hands—baskets of fruit, spiced game, jugs of ale, laughter soft as streams through their fields.

Three beautiful women, with braided hair and long dresses stepped forward holding baskets of mushrooms on their hips. They filled the crew's hands with as much as they could hold. The entire greeting seemed designed to overwhelm, to give more than one could accept, an abundance showered on a guest.

The River Ritual

The generosity paused as the crowd opened, revealing Olga, a frowning elderly woman who directed the men to a table where they could place their gifts. She spoke in a foreign tongue and pointed at the river, while shooing the villagers away. The crowds turned immediately and retreated to the tavern awaiting the completion of the men's bathing.

At the center of the village, the river flowed like a natural centerpiece, carved smooth into the canyon stone.

The crew listened to Olga's rapid, unfamiliar words, quickly realizing delay was not an option.

"I think it's part of a ritual," Steffan said quietly, already shrugging out of his sweat-soaked coat. He let it fall onto the rocks and looked to Olga for approval.

She watched closely.

"This too?" he asked, gesturing to his trousers as the others followed suit.

"Vso. Davai," Olga snapped, motioning sharply toward the water.

In that moment, she was more intimidating than anything they had encountered in the jungle.

Within minutes, the men stood waist-deep in the cold stream, shivering, uncertain of what came next. Olga paced the river edge like a drillmaster, tossing each of them a scented stone made of pumice.

She barked instructions, correcting their movements with sharp gestures, softening only when they complied correctly — her approval marked by a brief smile or a dry chuckle at their clumsiness.

Laughter drifted from villagers who understood her words. The men did not — but they understood the tone.

This was not humiliation.

This was inspection.

Bathing in the river was common here, though usually done privately. Today, it was enforcement.

A tailor arrived with fresh clothing and laid it out on the nearby table. Without ceremony, he gathered the crew's filthy leathers and carried them off, his face twisted in disgust.

Weeks of unwashed sweat and oil were more than offensive — Olga muttered sharply, gesturing toward the jungle. Such scents drew predators.

As she waved the men from the water, directing them to dress, she pointed them toward the tavern. Barra watched from his terrace above, half-shadowed in the canyon wall.

"Get them provisioned and get them off the island as soon as possible," he muttered to himself.

Stories and Warnings

The crew walked back to the tavern where all the villagers waited to ask them questions. Every seat in the tavern was filled, as others stood in the door to hear their stories. Steffan recounted their departure from Airovale, the mining operation and the great storm. His words painting pictures in their minds, as each man was served fresh ale. Their curiosity piqued when he spoke of Airovale and the Crescent Islands. The storm was almost a distraction from their interest in life in other villages.

Barra joined them later, after the crowds had thinned and the crew had a chance to eat and settle. As he entered the tavern, a subtle tension rose. Conversations narrowed. Some villagers chose their words more carefully; others spoke less or excused themselves altogether. Several left the room without explanation.

Barra was betrothed to Kira, daughter of Thalos—the elder who represented the fae of the island. The marriage was ceremonial, meant to preserve balance between the humans and the unseen powers that governed the land. It was no secret that Kira opposed the match. She spoke against it openly.

Barra's authority depended on appearances. Harmony, whether genuine or not, kept order.

"I saw the campfire from your crash site tonight," Barra said, pulling a chair to their table. "It's a wonder you're still alive."

"The storm devastated the fleet," Steffan replied. "We were very fortunate."

"To survive the storm is admirable," Barra interrupted, "But walking through the jungle alone?"

He shook his head once.

"That was some kind of mercy."

The crew stiffened.

"This island is not mapped like the forests where you're from," Barra continued, his voice steady, almost instructional. "Paths shift. Things move. What lets you pass once may not do so again."

Steffan started to respond, but Barra raised a hand.

"You were fortunate," he repeated. "Do not mistake that for safety."

The crew exchanged glances, unconvinced but listening.

"Some of our men will accompany you in the morning," Barra said. "They'll help carry provisions and assist with repairs. But, you will not return through the forest alone."

The silence that followed made it clear this was not a suggestion.

Steffan leaned forward, "We deeply appreciate everything you have done for us Barra, you've created an amazing village here."

Barra paused, then relaxed his posture. "I appreciate that, The Mystics are a generous people and Canyon Myst is a work in progress, but it's been home to me since birth."

"You were born here?" the aeronaut asked, surprised by the revelation.

"Yes, one of the few, actually." Barra began, as he reached for an ale from a passing maiden. "My father was a pirate who crashed his ship on the rocks, barely made it ashore. He and my mother tended one of the farms beyond the canyon and had me and my two brothers."

"Ah, so your whole family is here then?" the mechanic said in relief, "Everyone we've talked to seems to be apart from their homes."

Barra looked into his mug while speaking. "They left, my father was no farmer, so after my brothers were old enough, they packed up and set out to find a life more suited to his unique talents as a swordsman."

"But you stayed?" Steffan asked.

Barra set his mug on the table, and stood without answering. "Right, Olga has agreed to put you up for the night. Stay with her until I see you in the morning."

At that, Olga entered the tavern, smiling as though greeting old friends. Where Barra brought tension, she brought warmth—familiar, maternal, reassuring. The men felt as though they were being ushered into a grandmother's care rather than placed under watch.

She led them to her home in the canyon wall, a two story structure made from living trees, and cut timbers that connected into the caves. A row of hammocks were hung for them on the second floor, along with a pile of provisions and tools donated by the villagers for their journey. Baskets of bread and dried fruits, jugs of ale, and a crate of gears taken from old shipwrecks.

Olga continued speaking in her foreign language, pointing at pots and blankets, watching their faces for nods that they understood—although it was vaguely clear.

"No davai, spat," she said sweetly as she waved and exited the room.

For a moment, the crew felt renewed, welcomed, bathed, clothed, fed, and a little drunk as they tested the hammocks for comfort. The long day in the jungle had drained them of any energy, making it easy to sleep in minutes.

Steffan lay in his hammock, listening to the sound of the village outside. The hum of the waterfall, music in the tavern, and distant birds calling out in the jungle. It was an incredible place, and the people were like angels, providing for every need.

He looked over to see the mechanic and an aeronaut still awake as well. An unease pressed at the edges of their thoughts.

"Why didn't the people speak of their home—before Canyon Myst?" Steffan whispered to them in the dim light.

"You too?" The mechanic replied, "And, if they're shipwrecked too, wouldn't they want to return with us?"

"Maybe they don't trust us," the aeronaut muttered. "Maybe they just want us gone?"

"Or maybe," the crew mechanic said slowly, "They're hiding something they don't want us to know."

The thought lingered, heavier than the ale. Why had the villagers fed them like kings? Why clothe them? Why advise with such urgency to mend the hull and leave?

"Whatever it is, it must be in the jungle, otherwise why deny us to go there?" Steffan added.

The Midnight Path

After the other men had sunken into sleep. Steffan, the mechanic and the aeronaut decided to slip away in the darkness, slipping by Olga as she snored loudly.

Within minutes they had followed a path into the jungle, unseen, moving quietly. The trails split in multiple directions, Steffan chose the first as it was the most traveled, and led the men down a winding slope where a dirt road appeared.

They halted suddenly, when they saw a man with a lantern standing by the road, waiting for a horse-drawn cart to stop. It was Barra! He spoke briefly with a cloaked driver, accepting a small object that he put in his pocket. Their words were muffled, as they shook hands and the cart continued along the road.

Steffan motioned for the men to move back up the trail, silently, cautiously avoiding detection. They moved quickly, choosing a different path away from Barra.

They walked for an hour, as the jungle received them with an uncanny hush. No birds called, no insects sang. They began to notice trees on the trail where faces had been carved into the trunks—eyes closed, mouths sealed, sleepers imprisoned in wood on the path where they walked under the moon. It felt like a graveyard, or ceremonial place as the grass and vines were all cleared away.

They followed the roar of a waterfall until the faint laughter of women drifted from everywhere and nowhere. A shimmer broke the dark—first a flicker, then fleeting forms: fae, luminous and unearthly, ethereal visions appeared around them. Limpid wings caught the moonlight; their eyes held a strange charm, drawing the men into weightless surrender.

At the water's edge, a fairy sat on the roots of an ancient tree, clothed in exquisite flowers and leaves. Her hair was like spun gold, and her eyes sparkled as she lifted a hand, and from an overhead limb a massive tiger dropped soundlessly to the ground behind them. The tiger growled with its eyes fixed on the crew as it walked between them and lay next to the fairy. She looked at the men with curiosity and stilled the beast with a touch, like a hound awaiting command. She stroked its head, then with a final glance, both fairy and tiger moved back into the shadows of the bushes.

Silence closed in again, leaving only the crash of the falls. The aeronauts stood frozen until the mechanic whispered: "We need to leave."

By the time the men staggered back, dawn was only a few hours away. Their faces were pale, their voices hushed. Steffan wondered if it was the ale, causing them to see visions, but it was no dream, they knew it was real. They quietly returned to their hammocks, agreeing not to speak of the events to the others.

The Exchange

At dawn, the village was already stirring. The crew awoke as men appeared at their door, to carry the provisions to the crash site. The mood was different. Few words were spoken as the men headed downstairs where the entire village waited, with Barra standing at the front of the crowd.

The friendly faces had faded, their earlier warmth now tempered with something like pity. They looked at the aeronauts not as guests, but as men already condemned.

Barra stepped forward.

The crowd fell silent at once.

"Last night," he said, his voice calm but weighted, "some of you learned why the jungle is not a place for wandering."

A ripple moved through the villagers — not fear, but agreement.

"The fae guard Canyon Myst. We live here by their allowance." He gestured toward the trees. "Without that pact, the beasts would rule us. Not metaphorically. Literally."

Someone in the crew shifted.

Barra's gaze found the three men who had slipped away.

"You came here empty," he continued. "We fed you. Clothed you. Gave you tools. That was mercy — not obligation."

The word mercy landed hard.

"You will need to hunt. Repair your vessel. Mine for coal if you mean to leave." His mouth twitched. "The fae will show you where it is permitted. And where it is not."

He let the silence stretch.

"The island never gives," Barra said at last. "There is only exchange."

A trail of fireflies brightened at the jungle's edge, pulsing like a held breath.

"The sprites will guide you. My men will escort you to their leader on the far side." He turned, then paused.

Barra stepped close to Steffan and placed a hand on his shoulder — firm, possessive.

"Stay on the path," he said quietly. "You've already cost us goodwill. The fae were... displeased by your curiosity."

His grip tightened, just enough to hurt.

"You're alive because they chose restraint."

Barra leaned in and knocked into Steffan while walking away, showing his outrage.

Steffan was stunned. Nothing was as it seemed. What began as a warm welcome had become a dangerous game with unknown rules, and beings that only existed in fables, until now.

They began the journey to their ship unsettled, fearful, and more curious than ever. They walked for hours with a few villagers, carrying provisions for their crewmates, fireflies marking their path in silence—each man burdened with more questions than answers. The mechanic described what they had seen, but the villagers were silent, refusing to comment or explain the rules of Canyon Myst.

Steffan began to question his existence in the strange world. Was this all an illusion? Had they already died, and this the next existence? Or was there still a chance—to gather what they needed, repair their vessel, and journey home?

As they followed the trail, he looked past the fireflies, and wondered what dangers were restrained on the other side.

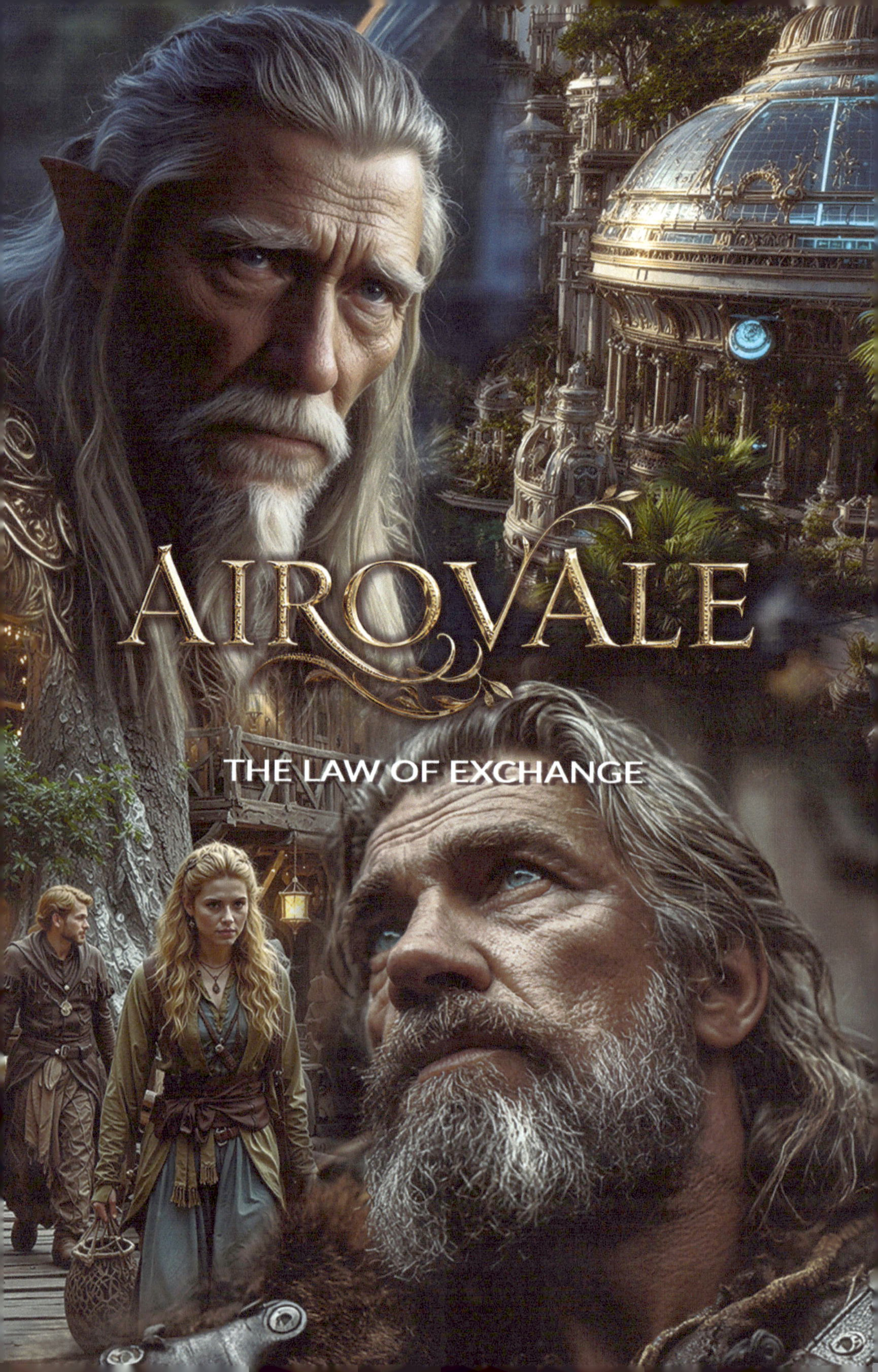

AIROYALE
THE LAW OF EXCHANGE

The Law of Exchange

Provisions and Secrets

By sunset, the crew emerged from the forest along with the villagers, arms laden with provisions. Their shipmates rushed to unburden them, elated at the sight of food, ale, and materials for repair. It was as though salvation itself had been carried in from the trees.

In the frenzy of celebration, Steffan stood at the edge of firelight, ale untouched in his hand, as he looked out at the field of fireflies encircling the camp, as questions swept through his mind.

"What else is waiting out there in the dark? How many?"

The engineer sat on a log by the campfire, quietly turning the tip of a stick in the glowing embers. He flinched noticeably when two of his crewmates laughed and stumbled into him, while telling a story.

"Sorry mate!" they apologized, as he forced a smile and walked away.

The aeronaut sat by himself on the top deck of the Nereid, looking into the trees. His imagination had been reshaped by what he saw at the sacred grounds.

"Is that one?" He thought to himself, squinting at a group of fireflies, wondering if another fairy would appear on the branches in the distance. He could still sense the glow of her face, and the sensation of surrendering to her beauty.

Those who remained in their hammocks the previous night were blissfully unaware of the discoveries revealed. And for now, the taste of ale drowned suspicion in the hearts of the crew. It was the first moment of joy since their departure from the Crescent Islands, and no one wanted to take that from the men. Fires were stoked, bread was torn, and goodwill passed from hand to hand as laughter rose against the evening sky.

Steffan walked back to the fire, making eye contact with the engineer and the aeronaut, acknowledging their silence. Steffan knew he had to update the captain—but not now, not openly.

Tales of Canyon Myst

The men of the village remained stoic, greeting the crewmen and listening to their versions of the crash stories told by Steffan. When the revel quieted, the captain pressed Steffan to share what they had seen. Their silence broke at last, and the tale spilled out.

They spoke of Canyon Myst, the village carved into canyon walls, and of the Mystics—humans and fae who lived in strange accord. They told of the beasts that prowled the wooded areas, and of the fae's power to command them.

Steffan pointed to the jungle and around the crash site, where fireflies hovered like a shield wall, protecting the men unaware. He stepped toward the glowing sentinels and noted how they shifted, pushing danger away. The village men confirmed the details and stressed the dangers of being in the jungle alone, warning of shifting pathways that moved without warning.

By the campfire, stories continued, the men listening as though the ground itself held secrets. The ale had loosened tongues, and the villagers spoke of sailors and aeronauts who had crashed, wrecked, or been swept ashore over the years—each arriving by chance, staying by enchantment. The Mystics cultivated the land, and the fae shielded them. It was a pact as old as memory.

The crew listened with clarity of mind. They would not linger. Repairs would begin in the morning, provisions stored, coal gathered.

Yet even as they resolved to escape, Barra's warning hung like iron chains in Steffan's mind: This island never gives—there is only exchange.

The Captain's Concern

Von Holt saw the trouble in Steffan's face and motioned for him to speak privately. They went aboard the Nereid and stepped into his cabin.

"We've had too many voyages together, old friend. I can see something is bothering you," Von Holt said as he pushed a chair toward Steffan.

Steffan sat and added the missing details of the story told to the men. He spoke of their suspicion of Barra, the encounter in the jungle with the stunning fairy and her tiger—then his voice changed.

"Aside from what must sound fantastic to you, there is something else," Steffan began.

"These people have an unnatural stillness that clings to them. Beyond their generosity, their contentment, they have no longing for home—no wish to return to the world beyond."

"What are they hiding?" the captain muttered.

"We thought the same thing—the others as well," Steffan replied. "But it's clear that being here is dangerous, and our protection is temporary."

The captain contemplated their situation. They had food now, raw materials for repairs, and the promise of assistance—enough to make their vessel sound again, enough to carry them home. Still, the contradiction gnawed at him. Why treat them so richly? Why urge them to leave quickly, but not seek passage themselves?

"And when do we meet this leader of the fae?" Von Holt asked, staring at a crude map of the island he had drawn from memory while landing.

Steffan stepped closer and made annotations on the map, murmuring to himself. "This is all jungle here. The village is wedged into a canyon due east, with waterfalls in several locations."

"They said we would be introduced on this side. I would think—soon," Steffan added, his eyebrows lifting in intrigue.

Von Holt nodded and suggested they return to the crew.

The Elder Arrives

They emerged from the gondola of the Nereid to hear one of the villagers singing by the fire. Von Holt stopped in his tracks.

"I've not heard that song since I was a boy," he said softly. "My great-grandmother used to sing it—same verses, same rhythm." His eyes welled with tearful memories.

Von Holt began singing along and walked to the villager, placing an arm around him in a familiar bond, as if they were old friends. The men sat in complete silence, hearing the captain sing for the first time and seeing him overcome with emotion. The villager looked at him with quiet confusion, then suddenly stopped singing. Von Holt continued alone, then paused before the next line.

A sound echoed in the distance, moving closer with time. It sounded like whispers of birds mixed with the wind. The trees stirred as the men startled, looking to one another for understanding. From the shadows of vines and leaves stepped Thalos, elder of the fae.

His long white beard matched his hair. Dragonfly-shaped wings extended from his back, slightly yellowed, shimmering as the firelight passed through them. While his escorts waited at the forest's edge, Thalos walked alone toward Von Holt. No one spoke, even the crackle of the fire seemed to calm in silence.

The crew sat in awe, mouths open, astonished at seeing a creature known only from legend. A hush fell over them, one by one each man stood.

"You are the captain," Thalos stated, already perceiving the crew around him.

"Von Holt," the captain replied, smiling awkwardly as he extended his hand.

Thalos reached out with both hands and held Von Holt's in a peaceful gesture. Energy passed through him and into the ground. Von Holt's smile faded, replaced by a sincere nod of humility.

The captain straightened, aware of his men's eyes upon him. He had never stood before a fae. "It is our honor to receive you," he said.

"The honor is ours," Thalos replied kindly. "I have come to guide you to the sacred caves, where you will find fire-stone for your ship and hunt to provision your journey. We will depart at first light."

"Wonderful!" Von Holt replied, nodding nervously to his men.

"Um—dine with us?" he added quickly. "You and your men as well. Please."

Stories of the Sunken City

Thalos hesitated, then inclined his head. A handful of fae males emerged, their wings catching the firelight and casting opalescent hues around the campfire. They listened as the crew spoke of Airovale, the great storm, and weeks adrift in vapors.

When the fae spoke, it was of the island. They told of an ancient city that had once stood proud upon these shores—a marvel of stone and wisdom, its towers consumed when fire spilled from the mountain's heart. What remained lay drowned beneath the great falls, entombed between flame and sea. The men shifted uneasily, in the silence between words, they heard it—distant thunder of water pouring down the nearby mountains, where an ancient city lay drowned.

The men marveled as Thalos spoke. He was slighter than the others, his back bent by centuries of life, yet his eyes were bright and his presence commanding. He carried himself not as a frail relic, but as one who had endured ages.

As he spoke, vapors of smoke formed between his hands—images of fairies and volcanoes curling into view, then fading into others. The men listened, mesmerized, asking questions until Thalos finally signaled his weariness.

The crew knew they would speak of him for the rest of their days. His motives matched the villagers': to assist the crew in mending their vessel and departing the island. Nothing more.

As Thalos prepared to withdraw for the night, the men instinctively rose, forming a line to express their gratitude. One by one they stepped forward—rough aeronauts unused to ceremony yet compelled by something deeper than protocol. Each man clasped Thalos's hand briefly, murmuring thanks, their voices thick with reverence.

When Aden's turn came, he hesitated. The orphan who had learned to make himself small, invisible in crowds, felt exposed standing before the fae elder. He extended his hand, conscious of the coal dust still beneath his nails.

Thalos took it—and held.

The contact lasted longer than with the others. A warmth spread through Aden's palm, traveling up his arm like liquid sunlight. For a heartbeat, the firelight seemed to brighten, casting Thalos's eyes in amber. The elder's grip tightened, not painfully, but with purpose—as though confirming something.

Thalos studied Aden's face, his gaze lingering on the worn aviator goggles hanging around the young man's neck. Something flickered in the ancient eyes—recognition, perhaps, or simply the kindness of one who had seen much.

"You carry more than leather and glass, young aeronaut," Thalos said quietly, his voice meant only for Aden. "Those who have no roots often grow the deepest."

Aden's throat tightened. No one had ever looked at him this way—as though seeing not what he lacked, but what he might become.

"My name is Aden, sir," he managed.

"Aden," Thalos repeated, as though testing the weight of it. "You remind me of someone long ago." A gentle smile touched his weathered features, and he released the young man's hand slowly.

The elder stepped back, signaling his weariness to the others. As the fae withdrew into the forest, vanishing with the rustle of leaves,

Aden remained rooted to the spot, his hand still warm where Thalos had held it.

Plans were made. At dawn they would walk with Thalos to the caves and hunting grounds. The embers faded to grey, and the aeronauts watched the forest edge with unease settling on their shoulders.

The three men gathered, looking around to ensure no one heard them.

Steffan paused, cautioned by how the bargain felt, "It's too narrow, too exact. Food, wine, and coal, even the repair parts, it seems so carefully measured."

"This is no gift," the mechanic muttered in agreement. "We're paying for it without knowing the price."

"Mates, maybe we're being paranoid. They mean us no harm, clearly they're just trying to get us home." The aeronaut added.

They looked toward the villagers and crew who were stretching out quietly by the fire.

The camp drifted into slumber—some on the open ground, others aboard the ship. Ale and exhaustion claimed them all.

Into the Sacred Caves

At dawn, Thalos and his escort returned. They guided the captain and a company of men into the forest along paths that darkened with every step. At last, the trees withdrew, revealing a carved archway crowned with runes, leading into a massive cave. The stone door—lined with forgotten symbols—had been split and pried open by living vines, its secrets torn wide like a wound in the mountain.

As the men entered, Von Holt remained outside with Thalos and his escorts.

"I see you are experienced miners. Take only what you need," Thalos said, his gaze fixed on the captain. "Beyond that, the island remembers."

Torches lit the way. Shadows danced across jagged walls as the men advanced, eyes widening at what the light revealed. Firestone—black rock veined with red—jutted from the walls. But beyond the coal, in hidden seams, gold and gems gleamed. Rubies, sapphires, crystals of impossible clarity winked like stars in the dark—wealth enough to stagger kings.

The captain thanked Thalos and pledged restraint as the fae departed. Then he entered the cave and felt unease coil in his chest. There was coal enough for the furnaces—but his men's gazes drifted to the brighter veins.

The Ungrateful Heart

They were miners, laborers of the earth who knew its language. At once they saw that fire-stone was the least of the treasures here. Murmurs spread.

"This is why they want us to leave," one hissed.

"They hoard it," another muttered. "Why share so freely unless they keep the true wealth for themselves?"

The captain tried to silence them, but the seed was planted, and the gratitude for the Mystics began to sound like suspicion and resentment.

Aden listened in silence, as he dug into the coal as instructed. The pickaxe penetrated the soft walls, sending rubble and dust onto his feet. Sweat began to drip into his eyes, as he searched his pockets for a kerchief. He pulled out a small stem with a leaf on it, and instantly remembered the apple Kateryna had given him in Airovale.

As the men around him spoke of treasure, he was taken back to the moment an apple was all he had, and even that was a gift that led him toward the *Nereid.*

"For good," he whispered to himself, remembering her smile as she placed it in his hand.

"What is gold worth on an island?" he said aloud.

The men halted for a moment, then dismissed him as naive.

Aden's thoughts were unchanged by their reaction.

He slipped the apple leaf back into his pocket, wiping the coal from his eyes with the sleeve of his jacket.

"A few days ago we were all starving, and now we have everything we wished for. Is your gratitude so fragile that it disappears on a full stomach?"

Words were quickly smothered in dust, sweat, and the rising clamor of tools. In the nights that followed, aeronauts smuggled gems from the caves, filling chests with glittering spoil while taking only a fraction of the fire-stone needed.

The fae observed from a distance and felt the imbalance begin to grow. The island stirred, calling on fate to intervene—to reward or punish. In the forests, sacred stones lifted above the hallowed grounds, hovering in silent warning, as though the island itself had begun to wake.

The fae elders were alerted and shook their heads in sad remembrance of times when the exchange was violated. None dared speak aloud what the signs foretold.

Thalos stood with the elders, and sighed in disappointment.

"There is no rescue for the ungrateful heart drowning willingly in the insatiable abyss."

AIROVALE
DECEPTIVE TIME

Deceptive Time

Treasures and Departures

Von Holt and Steffan studied every map they had in the captain's cabin, trying to determine their course home. They counted days in the wind while aloft in the storm, when the sun was at their back, and the faces of the moon. Steffan combed through the log, piecing the events into a direction.

"Maps! They are useless unless you know where you are at the start!" Von Holt shouted as he tossed them across his cabin.

Steffan traced a line with his finger. "We came in heading into the morning sun. If we reverse course and fly due west—"

"Two weeks to the Crescents, less with a tailwind," Von Holt finished, nodding with more confidence than the maps warranted.

"And if we're wrong?" Steffan asked quietly. "If we have to backtrack?"

Von Holt's jaw tightened, but he didn't answer. Instead, he stood and motioned for Steffan to follow him to the hold.

The mines were nearly stripped of gems and gold, with plenty of fire-stone remaining. The crews had filled every crate and bin with riches, yet still they continued to the mines, taking on the minimum coal needed to get home—or so they hoped.

The captain walked along the decks then went into the hold where stores of coal and gems were piled. Gold had been pressed into every available corner and crevice. Outside the ship, a few crates of coal and an enormous amount of gems waited to be loaded.

The men gathered, waiting for direction, all wanting the same outcome but unsure how to achieve it.

"How much coal do we need to reach the Crescents?" Von Holt asked.

Steffan hesitated. "Minimum? Assuming the direction is west, and the winds hold and we burn slow... maybe half of what we have now."

The crew exchanged glances. One spoke up. "Then why are we wasting half our space on coal?"

Von Holt interrupted, sensing challenge. "Because it's not just the space, it's the weight, you damned fool."

"The captain is right," Steffan added quickly. "And we should take on a full load of coal for insurance against the unexpected."

Von Holt looked at the gems stacked in the field by the ship, then at the sealed crates of Crescent copper they'd already hauled across the magnetic sea. A slow smile spread across his face.

"What if we dump the copper?" he said. "Make room for the gold there, and store the gems in the hold. We have twice the coal we need, as you said."

The men erupted in agreement, moving toward the crates on the Nereid's deck.

"Hide it in the fields," Von Holt ordered. "We don't want to arouse suspicion among the Mystics. And leave your tools in the mine—we won't need them once we depart."

The captain grinned as he walked back to his cabin, feeling he had shown clever leadership.

Steffan trailed behind him, closing the door once they were inside.

"Captain, you know gold is twice the weight of copper," Steffan said, keeping his voice level. "And we're guessing we should head west based on theory, not maps. What if we're going the wrong way?"

"Watch your tone, first mate." Von Holt shuffled through the discarded maps on his desk without looking up. "The sun rises the same here as anywhere else. West is the answer, and we'll be fine. But if you want to fill the hold with coal instead of a life-changing amount of wealth, you'll find the crew hard to manage."

"I'm not suggesting we take on coal alone, but at least enough for insurance if we have to backtrack!"

"Insurance is for cowards!" Von Holt snapped.

Steffan looked at the ceiling in frustration, his hands resting on his hips as he took a long breath. "We still need to think about departure. Repairs are almost done and we're filling up fast with nothing we can eat."

Von Holt's expression shifted, the certainty draining from his face. "Aye," he said quietly. "And no one wants to go through starving again."

As each day had passed the captain had delayed departure to take on all they could carry home. He had given in to the spirit that infected his men—only treasure mattered, and there was no limit to their hunger. Some crates were replaced with clothing and spare canvas sewn into lightweight sacks filled to the brim. The hold, usually filled with coal, had been sectioned off with a space for each man and his share of the riches.

Soon they would depart, hoping the fae would not notice their clandestine efforts. When the fae visited each day, the men brushed coal on their faces and clothing to show their mining took a long time to complete. Entering the cave was forbidden to the fae, allowing the hoax to continue without suspicion—or so they thought.

"Thalos said we could hunt as long as they provided the guardians, if we start now, we should have enough to provision the trip." Von Holt surmised.

"I'll set it up." Steffan replied as he stepped out of the cabin.

The Hunt

The next morning, Aden was relieved to be one of the three chosen for hunting. His time mining coal in the caves exposed the dark greed in the hearts of his crewmates. He fetched his bow and quiver and met the captain in front of the ship where Thalos and a gathering of fairies stood. Aden arrived, his blond hair falling untamed across his brow, his eyes sharp but shadowed as he looked at the fairies with wonder.

The three men were told the best areas for game. Thalos stood before them, his eyes moving across the crew members, then pausing deliberately on Aden.

"Each of you will have a guardian," Thalos announced. He gestured to the fae who stood waiting, then his gaze settled on his daughter. "Kira, you will accompany Aden."

The other fae exchanged glances. Kira's wings fluttered—a barely concealed flash of displeasure. She looked at her father with quiet protest in her eyes.

The fairies looked at their pairings with contempt and disappointment. Thalos had insisted on the act of goodwill, so they obeyed out of respect for him. Kira moved with restless grace, her blue-eyed gaze fixed ahead, her translucent wings casting shifting patterns of light in the morning sun. Her reluctance was obvious. Thalos's eyes narrowed.

Thalos knew his daughter would do as he asked, but her tendency to push back and resist was in her blood, a trait her deceased mother was also known for. She was royalty among the fae, and she resented actions based on principle or station, especially the announcement of her betrothal to Barra in the village.

As instructions were completed, Thalos departed and the other pairs walked in their respective directions, leaving Kira and Aden in awkward silence as they stepped toward the tree line.

"I'm Aden," he said at last, his voice uncertain.

"Kira," she answered shortly, eyes narrowing toward the horizon. Her steps quickened, impatiently wanting to be finished with the task.

"You look dirty," she said condescendingly, her eyes avoiding him.

He patted his clothing for a moment as clouds of soot puffed into the air in her direction.

"Better?" he said calmly as she grimaced in disgust.

"Are you any good with that bow?" she asked, looking intently around the grass as it became deeper.

Aden's jaw tightened. "I hit what I aim for."

"Lots of practice on a zeppelin?" she teased.

He shook his head. "If you miss, you go hungry."

She found herself weighing him against Barra. Barra boasted endlessly of his sword skill, but he had never known hunger. Aden's words were spare, practical—truth, not pride.

"I guess we will see," she said.

Aden sensed her contempt. She was toying with him for amusement, indifferent to successful hunting. His eyes followed her movements when she wasn't looking. Her translucent wings shimmered, illuminating her glowing skin, enticing lips and stormy blue eyes. The wind seemed to caress her hair back as she walked.

She cannot possibly know how beautiful she is, he thought.

Kira faked a cough and waved her hand in front of her mouth. "You smell like fire-stone."

"That's because I've been in the caves for three days, working. But you wouldn't know anything about that," he said without reservation.

Kira went silent, taking in his words, unsure if they were deserved.

"Is Thalos your father?" Aden asked abruptly, sensing their familiarity earlier.

"Yes, why?" Kira replied, intrigued.

"Well, that makes sense," he muttered.

Kira stopped in her tracks, unsure how to handle disrespect. Humans never spoke to her this way.

"Don't talk about my father!" she said, reversing the insult as a defense.

"Your father is amazing; I have complete respect for him," Aden replied while continuing to walk ahead.

"Then why ask..." Kira started.

Aden interrupted, "Because you're a princess, entitled, spoiled and annoying, just like the royals back home."

"You would need my respect for your opinion to matter," Kira snapped, internally realizing she had never been labeled so harshly.

But Aden wasn't listening. He had walked ahead into the brush, and stopped suddenly, crouching, silently reaching for an arrow as he loaded his bow.

A rustle stirred in the high grass. Aden began taking aim, sighting the striped shoulders of a large white tiger in the shadows.

"Wait!" Kira shrieked. "Not food! Rabbits, deer, foxes—those are yours. This one is sacred."

The tiger stepped from the grass, revealing its massive size, it was the largest animal Aden had ever seen, with teeth the length of fingers, and a growl that shook the ground.

Kira fearlessly stepped between them, moving toward the striped giant, reaching without hesitation to scratch beneath its chin. The beast rumbled low, crouching as Kira whispered playful words in a language Aden had never heard. Its eyes softened, lids closing, a deep purr rolling through its chest like distant thunder. Then the great cat settled into the grass, soothed into sleep.

Aden lowered the bow slowly, disbelief in his eyes. Now he understood the need for a guardian.

Kira stood and walked onward, catching the disbelief in Aden's eyes.

Aden walked quicker to catch up, speaking in an excited whisper, "Are there more like that?"

"Thousands," she said, knowing there were only a few sacred tigers on the island.

She purposely walked faster, as he quickened his steps. The light moved through her wings as she swayed ahead of him, dressed in an ornate work of lush leaves and flowers. His thoughts betrayed his stern words.

"I had a cat like that once… smaller," he said dryly, creating a shape between his open hands.

Kira laughed, louder than expected. The sound surprised even her. "Ah, so you're an archer and a comedian. How did I get so lucky?"

"I don't know. It might be your looks, but definitely not because of your personality," he said.

Kira blushed, her mouth hanging open at the confidence of his insult—or was that a compliment?

She suppressed her smile, keeping her face angled away from him as the path blurred into limbs and rocks.

Shifting Paths

They wandered deeper, past groves and markers into woods where the villagers warned paths shifted without warning. Here, vines draped like veils, streams tangled through stone, and the air grew heavy with secrecy.

"And your father?" Kira asked sincerely.

"I never met him; he flew off before I was born and never returned. He didn't even know my mother was pregnant."

Kira's voice softened. "So your mother raised you alone?"

"For a while, she passed when I was five, and after that I had to make it on my own," Aden replied without thinking how it sounded.

"Only five...?" Kira repeated aloud, imagining the desperation of an innocent child in such a dangerous place as the cities she had heard the villagers talk about.

"I was lucky. I had already learned how to find food, and places to sleep at night. So..." Aden said confidently, while shrugging his shoulders.

"My mother died a year after I was born. I became terribly ill and she traded her years to heal me." Kira sighed, her voice softening momentarily, "There is so much I want to ask her about the wedding and life."

Kira explained the details of her fate—a forced union with the human leader in the village.

"The ceremony is next month. The entire island will gather around the waterfall in the human village. We say vows to each other and then to the pact, and then there is a feast that lasts for three days."

Aden asked, "Sounds...beautiful, are you excited?"

Kira hesitated. "It's actually not me that is supposed to be married. There was another elder's daughter, Vivian, she was next in the line. But she left the island years ago on a ship that never returned. It was quite the scandal back then."

Aden nodded. "So... again, lucky you?"

Kira's face flushed with anger, gritting her teeth as her emotions unlocked. "Yes! Lucky me! The prize that unites fae and humans, sustaining the sacred pact. The envy of every fairy!"

Aden remained silent, looking in her eyes.

"You must think I'm ungrateful, what was that word you used, entitled?" Kira continued.

Aden disagreed, shaking his head. "No. Actually I was thinking, the color in your eyes is quite spectacular when you're angry, and if this future husband is smart, he'll annoy you just to see more of it."

"You are bad!" Kira shouted while laughing, her voice echoing in the woods as she blushed again. She calmed down and wiped tears from her eyes.

Aden grinned. "So, is he smart? Tell me about him."

Kira tried to list Barra's virtues. "He has a strength, a commanding presence, but honestly, I have concerns about him. He gets insanely jealous of my friends, who I talk to, and he has a craving to be feared."

"I know men like that," Aden began. "Those violent types were in and out of prison back home. But I'm sure he's a good man if they made him their leader, right?"

"Right," Kira agreed quickly.

An awkward silence followed, there were no words to comfortably continue discussion of the wedding. The path ahead began to descend toward a river in the distance.

She studied the goggles he wore. They intrigued her, like a sacred heirloom that would be handed across generations of fae, this was his equivalent.

Aden noticed her gaze and pulled the goggles over his head and held them out. "You like these? You can try them on..." he said.

"Oh, no! I mean, I'd love to, but I can't... they will burn me for sure!" Kira replied as she distanced herself from his reach.

Aden's eyes grew large in disbelief. "Burn you?" he asked as he looked at his goggles with uncertainty.

"Yes, cold iron is dangerous for the fae. We keep a distance from humans to be safe from it," she cautioned.

"But you're wearing a necklace?" Aden pointed at the pendant hanging around her neck.

"Oh, right. Gold isn't harmful, as long as it's pure," she replied.

"I had no idea." Aden pulled his goggles back over his neck, turning them behind and out of sight.

He looked down at his clothing, all the metal clasps and buckles shining in light coming through the trees.

Aden rolled his shoulder to remove his quiver, taking a wide cloth tucked inside, tearing it into strips. "I must look like a hot stove to you."

"No, it's fine. I'm used to Barra, he's covered in swords and..." Kira watched as Aden wrapped every buckle in cloth, pulling them tightly in place. "We should keep going, it's fine, really..."

She walked ahead of him as he finished the last buckle.

Aden stood up, slipping the quiver over his shoulder and walking quickly to catch up.

"Much better," he said with a nod.

"How is it better?" Kira smiled, shaking her head.

Aden paused. "...Just in case."

Kira tilted her head. "In case of what exactly?"

"In case you... bump into me?"

Kira shook her head, suppressing her smile. "Oh, so I'm clumsy now?"

Aden walked ahead. "Maybe not, but you're definitely blushing."

Kira felt the warmth in her face. He was right.

They began to navigate a narrow path in silence. She began to contrast Barra against her father, who ruled by wisdom and presence, not force, as they continued their walk.

"You remind me of my father," she said. "Not in years, but in character. He also makes me laugh when I'm upset."

She thought of Barra's hands—how they gripped her wrist too tight when he was angry, how his touch always felt like ownership, not affection. Their conversations were always about ruling, not family. His constant wearing of swords and buckles gave her excuse not to embrace him.

Aden had pulled his goggles away without her asking, wrapped every buckle, protecting her from harm she'd barely explained. Such a small gesture. It shouldn't matter this much. But to her it felt like revelation, a message to open her eyes.

Aden walked in silence, thinking of his interaction with Thalos. The energy her father carried when speaking with the crew at the campfire. His stories of the island long ago had fascinated them all.

"How old is he?" Aden asked, innocently.

"Barra?" Kira replied.

"No, Thalos, your father." He insisted.

"Oh, it is not polite to ask such things," Kira replied gently, relieved not to speak of Barra.

Aden hesitated, preparing to apologize, but she softened. "It's alright—you didn't know. Our lives are measured in generations, not days or months. My father has seen the most generations. He was born here after the great eruption, when there were so few—fae or humans. I think it must have been lonely for them." Her voice faded into whispers.

"He told us about that last night… the whole island was like a volcano?" Aden asked.

"Not exactly. It was more like a mountain, with the most amazing city ever known. They had ships that dove beneath the sea, and towers of stone, with windows set in precious gems that caught the light and changed the colors. Nothing like the tree-villages we have now."

Aden thought of the mines, where his crewmates filled crates with glittering stones instead of coal. "Tell me, if jewels are so precious here," he asked quietly, "why does no one wear them?"

Kira's gaze flickered, almost amused. "Gems are just decoration—no different than the flowers in my hair."

"What about your home? Is it a great city?" she asked at last.

Aden spoke of Airovale—of alleys and shadows, of hunger and cold, of a boy who gave his last scrap of bread to a stray kitten that never left his side. His words carried no boast, only memory, concluding with his decision to work aboard the zeppelin. A decision influenced by a pair of aviator goggles around his neck. His mother gave them to him as a child, with the story they belonged to his father.

Kira grew quiet, realizing Aden was alone in the world, and had never known the sense of home she had taken for granted. "I can't imagine such a life. But to feel alone, even in crowded streets... that is a sensation I know too well, especially when everyone has a purpose for you that is self-serving."

Aden was unsure how to ask the obvious. "So, this wedding, is it... forced?"

"Not forced, but expected. I mean it's an honor, and I'll be the good wife, but without love, it feels like it will be a burden or a prison," she said, wishing to change the subject.

They walked in silence for a time, the forest deepening around them. Kira's eyes fixed toward the distant sound of water rushing through stone. A mischievous glint touched her expression.

"Would you like to see the ancient city?" she asked, her voice low, conspiratorial. "It lies beneath a forbidden river."

"Um, sure. But I'm supposed to bring back..." he began.

Kira interrupted him, "Oh we'll have enough time for hunting later," as she started to run toward the sound of the falls.

Beneath the Falls

The river called them onward. They waded knee-deep, then waist-deep, the roar swelling as they drew near the mouth of the falls. Mist clung to their skin, sunlight shimmering across the river's flow.

"Where are we going again? I don't see anything here except the river," Aden said, speaking over the water's churn.

She flashed to a memory of secret confessions by her friends who had dared to visit the ancient city.

Beneath the waterfall's edge, Kira's steps slowed. She turned to him, her voice hushed by the waterfall as they stood facing each other. She moved closer to him as she confessed this was her first attempt.

"I just know the legends, but I have never gone beneath," she said. "It takes both fae and human to summon the sphere. Alone, no one can do it."

Aden was unsure what she was proposing, but her eyes sparkled in a way that filled him with anticipation of what was about to happen. She slipped her hands on his shoulders, nervously.

Aden interrupted, "Not even with Barra?"

Her gaze hardened. "Never with him. Not now. Not ever," she said, punching his arm playfully in protest. "We just need to..."

She faltered, her hand hovering near his face. "If Barra knew—if my father—"

Aden started to pull back. "We don't have to—"

"No." Her fingers found his jaw, trembling. "I've spent my whole life doing what's expected."

She drew him closer. "Just once, let me choose."

Silence lingered. Then she guided his face toward hers.

Their lips met—brief, tender, but potent as fire. At once a sphere of air shimmered into being, encircling them. Energy rippled like starlight dust, flowing from them both, sealing them within the sphere.

Kira drew back, her hand brushing the curve of the bubble. "It worked!" she whispered. "Only fae and human can make this!"

Aden watched in amazement. Embracing Kira, they sank beneath the veil of the waterfall, plunging safely into the depths. Enclosed in an enchanted bubble of air, the current swept them through sunken walkways, into a city sealed by water and time. Walls rose around them, vast and bioluminescent, carved with glyphs of fae and man standing side by side—sharing hearths, councils, and harvests now lost to memory.

Deeper still, a great chamber opened. Its walls bore mosaics etched with symbols that pulsed as though alive. They stepped from the sphere, eager to explore the vast space where the blue water flowed only over their feet, and the air tasted of mist and magic.

The stone walls glistened, marked with carvings so old they seemed to shift with the moving light. At the edge of the cave, an elaborate tunnel yawned, its carved rim spilling a glowing mist that faded into the water below.

"I've seen similar markings in the sacred caves," Aden said as he looked across the chamber.

Kira paused, her hand hovering above one of the etched symbols. "These are like the ones in the village," she murmured. "But older... much older."

Aden stepped on a ledge to read the carvings above him more clearly. He touched the corner of a rune and a tunnel at the edge of the cave began to hum, a shimmer pulsing as a deep vibration shook the chamber.

The stone burned hot beneath his hand, glyphs flaring white, mist pouring from the tunnel's mouth like breath from a waking beast.

Kira seized his wrist, pulling him back sharply. The glow snapped shut, the hum collapsing into silence.

Her breath trembled. "I don't know what that was... but it wasn't meant for us."

Aden nodded in agreement.

The Exchange

The carvings responded to Kira's touch in a faint glow. Symbols lit one by one—a sun, a mountain, an island encircled by waves. As she hovered her hand over each symbol, the glyphs around the tunnel flickered in response.

Aden's breath caught. "It feels alive."

Kira followed the etched markings, trying to read them, but the symbols danced, changing even under her gaze.

"Can you read it?" Aden asked, his eyes tracing the glyphs.

"This is the lost language," Kira replied. "I remember ancient texts of it in the library at Sibhruion, but I only remember fragments."

"Sibhruion?" Aden's brow furrowed as he tried to pronounce the word.

"The fae palace," she replied, trying to pronounce the meanings of the glyphs.

They studied each glyph, matching the carvings on the wall with those around the tunnel.

Kira hesitated. "This is ancient magic—we should be cautious."

She turned and placed her hand upon a stone mosaic, and light surged through the cracks, like liquid fire, emitting a warm glow.

Her eyes widened as she traced the symbols, speaking them aloud, hauntingly.

"One day... given..." She squinted, moving her finger to the next glyph. "One year... taken away..." Another pause, her voice dropping. "Beyond?" She went back, checking her reading against what she remembered from the library.

"One day given, one year taken beyond the island shores," she concluded.

"Is it a warning about staying on the island?" Aden asked, remembering how the crew felt they were rushed to leave.

Her voice faltered. "No—it's a warning for those who leave. A day here, has been a year!"

The words hung in the water-touched air.

Aden's mind went blank for a heartbeat, then raced. He started counting—first on his fingers, then in his head, then aloud because the numbers felt too impossible to keep silent.

Kira's hand found his arm.

"How many days have you been here?" she asked, though she already knew the answer, needing to hear it spoken again to believe it.

Aden accounted for each day, dreading the weight of days to years in the final sum.

"We landed, then two days to the village and back, mining for three, and today makes..." He looked at Kira, his face draining of color. "Seven."

"Seven days," Kira breathed.

"Seven years." Aden's legs nearly gave out. He gripped the stone wall for support. "Seven years we've been gone."

The faces of the crew came to him, one by one. Ivan, who'd shown him a worn sketch of his daughter on their second night aboard—three years old, gap-toothed and laughing. She'd be ten now. Would she even remember her father's face?

Hansel, the oldest of the crew, talked endlessly about his wife's bread, how she'd promised to bake his favorite when he returned. Seven years of promises, of waiting, of wondering if he was dead.

Young Quinn, barely of age, whose wife had been heavy with their first child when he left. "Just one voyage," he'd said. "One good haul and I'll never leave again." That child would be in school now. Walking, talking, calling someone else papa, perhaps.

"Their children..." Aden's voice cracked, remembering how his father never returned. He reached and touched the goggles around his neck, wishing to spare the crew's children from his childhood fate. "The plan was to provide, not abandon."

He reflected on crewmates who'd given the orphan thief a second chance when they could have left him to starve in Airovale. The men who'd shown him how to work the ropes, who'd shared their rations during the storm, who'd clapped him on the back and called him part of the crew.

They'd been taking their time. Days spent mining every gem, every nugget of gold. Treasures that were supposed to save their families, make their sacrifices worthwhile. And every additional hour they'd delayed was weeks stolen from the people waiting for them.

"We need to leave. Now." The words came out hollow.

They rushed back to the depths, and kissed once more, as the bubble carried them upward, bursting upon the surface with a rush of air. Aden staggered toward the bank, water streaming from him as he rushed back along the path toward the ship. Every second was theft from the lives of the crew's children.

The Cost of Truth

Kira kept up with him, her heart torn. At the edge of the woods they saw the Nereid, tethered and loading.

They halted, breathless. Aden looked into Kira's eyes as she reached for him. His body shook with exhaustion.

"Aden, I..." She put her hands on his shoulders, saying his name for the first time.

"I have to tell them." He looked toward the ship. "They need to leave. Now."

"Then stay. Stay here with me."

He turned back to her, the words catching in his throat. "I don't want to leave you."

"This is madness," Kira breathed. "I've known you for hours—"

"I know."

"And I'm promised to another—"

"I know." He took her hand. "But when you look at me like that... when you speak—" He couldn't finish.

"I feel it too," she whispered. "More understood in one day than I have in centuries."

"But Barra—your father—" The weight of it pressed against his chest.

"I don't want Barra. I want you." She said it like a confession. Like breaking an oath.

Aden cupped her face. The Nereid waited in the distance. Every second he delayed cost the crew's families weeks. But standing here, with Kira trembling in his hands—

"I've lived more today than in my entire life," he said quietly. "Let me warn them. Then we'll figure out the rest. Together."

She nodded, tears streaming. They kissed once more, breathing each other in like a promise made.

"I'll go with you," she whispered.

Then a branch snapped.

Footsteps followed—villagers of Canyon Myst, carrying provisions toward the zeppelin. They were close. Too close. And at the back of the line stood Barra.

They had seen everything, and he had heard every word.

Aden took Kira's hand and they ran toward the Nereid, choosing action over hesitation, truth over fear—while the consequences of their newfound love closed in behind them.

AIROVALE
THE DUEL

The Duel

The Warning

Aden tore through the field of high grass, his warning about the time paradox still burning in his throat while the earth rushed beneath him as though it, too, urged him forward. He felt Kira's hand leave his as she lifted into the air, turning to face Barra and his men.

"Keep going!" she said, her voice fading behind him.

Aden looked back, concerned for her protection, but her confidence with wild tigers entered his mind, and he knew she could summon any defense. Her feet landed firmly in the open meadow, hands at her side, in a defiant stance.

Ahead, the tethered zeppelin loomed against the sky, a few crewmen clustered near the captain, who made eye contact with Aden as he approached. Aden's legs burned for rest, yet he drove harder, desperate to reach them before the truth slipped too far from grasp.

Barra pushed forward from the rear of the line. He had watched in silence until now.

He surged ahead, shoving past his own men as they approached with baskets meant for the *Nereid*. With sharp, violent motion, he struck the gifts aside. Fruit scattered across the grass. Wine skins burst as they hit the ground, soaking into the earth.

The gesture was unmistakable.

The goodwill of their welcome was over.

Barra looked at Kira as his eyes ran cold, a fury she had never seen in him before. His voice cut sharp, louder than wind or water, as he argued vehemently with Kira.

"This won't be good," Von Holt muttered as he and Steffan took in the scene. "Get the men out of the mines. We may need every hand."

Steffan ran, knowing it would take time to gather the crew. Barra's distant accusations rang like an indictment, dragging every warning about the island back into sharp focus.

Aden rushed up the gangplank, steadying himself on the ropes, his voice rasping from hard breathing. The captain looked Aden over, a quiver full of arrows and no hunter's bounty in his hands. Only fear, urgency, and the grim knowledge, this was bad news.

Von Holt assumed they had been discovered in some forbidden intimacy—enough to spark violence. His jaw tightened as Aden caught his breath.

"What madness brings you running back like this?" the captain growled, though even he felt the unease. "If you tried something with that elder's daughter, we're all dead."

Aden shook his head, clutching his knees, forcing the words out between ragged breaths. "We've stayed too long... the island... each day here is a year beyond!"

The captain hesitated, watching the faces of the crew, and they all understood it at once, "That's why they want us to leave!"

The crew exchanged looks, whispers rising like restless birds.

Von Holt looked toward the path to the mines. Steffan was out of view but would return with the rest of the men soon.

"And this?" Von Holt asked, pointing toward Barra's screaming in the distance.

"We kissed." Aden bowed his head, knowing how it sounded.

Von Holt paused, his eyes drifting to where Kira stood—defiant, stunning, arguing with Barra. He looked back at Aden, something between amusement and resignation crossing his face.

"Of course you did," he muttered. Then his expression hardened. He turned to the crew who had gathered around. "Grab your tools. We might be fighting today."

The men's eyes met in silent conference. Most of their tools were still at the mines, abandoned for the weight of gold. They shuffled around the deck, looking for a suitable option—wanting to cast off rather than fight.

The Duel

Kira stood at the forest's edge, the last glow of sun catching her hair like fire. Barra was upon her, eyes blazing, his chest heaving as though betrayal itself had struck him in the gut.

"How could you? Here, in the forest, in the arms of that outsider? Before your people, before me?"

Barra paced before his men, pointing at Kira, accusing her of deception—of betraying him, the fae, the village itself.

"A few hours with that castaway," Barra spat, "and you're ready to throw everything away?"

His words and judgment were harsh, and Kira endured them as long as they bought Aden time. His men stood silently behind Barra; it felt as though his words were for them, not her.

"There was nothing to throw away," Kira shot back. "This was an arranged nightmare—one that benefited only you."

Barra froze. Then his voice dropped, tight with something far more dangerous than anger.

"You don't even know the damage you've done today."

Kira watched him closely, his eyes held no pain—he wasn't grieving, he was performing, preparing a defense to justify the fury of a man whose pride bled in front of an audience.

The pity of the villagers felt like knives to Barra. If he faltered, he lost more than Kira. He lost respect, authority, and the future bride that assured him his place as chief of the village.

"You are betrothed to me, by your father, and you will obey!" Barra growled.

Kira's face did not soften. She stood as though rooted to the earth, defiance flickering in her gaze. "There will be no wedding, and I will never obey you," she said evenly.

He drew steel, twin blades flashing in the dying sunlight. He lifted his hands, trembling with the need to strike, yet knowing a blow against her would ignite more than scandal. It would bring war with the fae.

Kira squeezed her fists, sending a call to her tiger in the distant jungle.

Barra turned his eyes toward the zeppelin. "I'll deal with you and your father later."

The murmur of onlookers fed Barra's rage. His mind spun in anger mixed with jealousy. Aden had to die; it would solve everything and satisfy his thirst for revenge. He pushed past Kira, his men in tow, raging toward the zeppelin, swords glinting as he reached the shadow of the *Nereid.*

"You have violated a sacred pact," his voice thundered. "Our laws demand you face me in a duel!"

Villagers hurried after, their faces a mix of shame and fear. There was no such law, but Barra felt he could rebuild his dignity by striking Aden down in front of his people. His eyes went red with tunnel vision to restore his assurance of power.

Von Holt stepped to the gangplank. "Easy there, brother. You can't have him, and you can't take us all either."

The sound of the rest of the crew arriving filled the distance as they appeared from the path behind Barra's men.

One of the villagers leaned close to Barra and whispered, "We're outnumbered. Let the fool go, and the problem is solved."

Barra calculated the outcome in his favor, scripting a response to restore himself in words projecting strength.

"Coward!" Barra shouted. "You touched her. You will die!"

Kira wept. She had followed and stood near the *Nereid,* watching Aden, afraid he would depart and leave her to the doom of marriage to a monster.

Barra looked and saw her sobbing, knowing she would never cry such tears for him. But if Aden left, he could shame his memory as abandonment, proof the outsider was never worth her tears.

"I see..." Barra said, his voice lowering in dark bitterness. "A martyr I'll never be rid of. Go on then, Captain, take your men and never return."

The villagers opened to allow the rest of the crew to board the ship. Steffan and the men stepped quickly, realizing they had to lift off quickly, unprepared but necessary.

Barra felt his pride returning. He had defeated his enemy, regained his respect, and could blame Aden for running in fear of him. It was better than taking his life. It took his memory as well.

"I accept," Aden said firmly from the deck as the last man boarded.

The captain, thinking he had solved the fight, was astonished.

"Are you a damned fool, boy?" Von Holt jabbed. "He's letting us go. That's the end of it."

Aden stepped to the gangplank and walked off the ship.

"I'm staying, and if that requires a duel, then I accept," he said bravely.

"Aden, no!" Kira shouted, knowing Barra was the most skilled swordsman on the island.

Von Holt considered the outcomes and turned to Steffan. "We're wasting time here. Prepare to launch."

Steffan echoed the captain's command as the gangplank retracted into the deck. Ropes were pulled, tethers cut, and the engine bellowed a black cloud, roaring to life. The crew hung by the rail, watching as they abandoned Aden to his chosen fate, lost time weighing on their minds, and dreams of returning wealthy awaiting.

The *Nereid* engines continued to churn as it creaked under its own weight to lift from the ground, offering a distraction as Barra charged Aden, giving no time for him to use his bow. The crew cheered for Aden, watching from above as he reacted from exhausted impulse and twisted away from Barra's blades. The Nereid began to lift, floating above the ground as the last line was cut, carrying the crew above the field where the outcome of the fight continued to unfold.

Barra swung as he lost his balance, grazing Aden's shoulder. The villagers shouted, eager to see Barra defeat the outsider who broke their traditions and hallowed laws. Kira cried, hovering above the fight, determined to help, to conjure magic, a force to protect Aden.

She could see the faces of the men on the Nereid, cheering for Aden but none offering to stay and defend him. It was her fault this had happened, she tightened her fists, sending an energy burst through the jungle, a silent plea that made every predator rush toward her.

The crew of the Nereid, saw trails in the high grass converging from all directions toward the unaware crowd.

"What is that?" Von Holt said aloud.

"Everything we were protected from, unleashed." Steffan said as he swallowed hard at the hidden dangers of Canyon Myst.

Kira hands bled as she squeezed her fists harder, her fingernails cutting into her palms as the terror of hungry beasts listened and moved in to destroy all but Aden.

Aden looked past Barra and recognized the stripes of the tiger he had seen earlier as it stalked toward them. Unaware there were dozens more around them.

He feared Kira would suffer his fate for breaking the pact with humans. He turned and looked up at her hovering above them, her eyes glowing as her fists clenched in resolve.

"Kira, no! It's me against him. Stay out of it!" he shouted, his eyes tensing as Barra turned to run at him again.

Kira opened her hands, her body shaking as she gasped to release the animals from her bidding, one by one they diverted and returned to the woods.

The men on the Nereid watched her in amazement, as the animals retreated. Their shouts continuing as the duel continued below. Kira was enraged by their duplicity in leaving Aden, when he had tried to save them from their own greed. She raised her hand toward the ship, releasing the energy that welled within her, sending a contrary wind to labor their efforts aloft.

Barra pressed forward, roaring insults, threatening punishment for Kira afterward, slashing wildly. He spoke not only to Aden but to the crowd, desperate to reclaim dignity before their eyes.

Aden had lived too long on the streets of Airovale to be cowed. With speed born from survival, he caught Barra's wrist, wrenching the blade from his hand. Then he struck to disarm the second sword, deeply cutting Barra's left arm.

Aden halted, holding one of Barra's swords. The other sword lay on the ground, where Barra's blood oozed into the grass. Aden stepped back, granting Barra a chance to reconsider his wrath before bleeding out.

"It's over," Aden commanded. "Enough."

The crowd pulled back, stilled by Aden's grace toward his opponent. He could have taken advantage, but he chose to seek peace, the way of the island.

Aden looked toward Kira as she wiped her tears. Barra sank to one knee, his arm drenched from his own blood, feeling the crowd turn and favor Aden.

Kira made no effort to conceal her affection for Aden, her tears bore testament to her devotion.

Barra watched in silent rebuke as his plans slipped away like the blood from his body. Although he knew he did not love her, he envied Aden for winning her heart without power or prestige. Then something inside him, went dark.

He rushed to his feet, extending his right arm to grip Aden's throat, squeezing with brutal force while knocking Aden onto his back. The crowd gasped as Barra drove himself onto the sword still in Aden's hand. The blooded edge extended out of Barra's armor as he held on to Aden, slipping to his knees then rolled to the side.

His eyes watered and bulged as he fought for breath. He felt his life leaving his body, the sorrow of his once-great plans fading into despair, knowing his blind wrath had manifested his own doom.

"You think you beat me boy?" He coughed, spitting blood on Aden's face.

"Life for—"

He took a final breath, cursing Kira and Aden as blood gurgled from his mouth.

Condemned

"Life for a life," a villager in the crowd said.

"It wasn't murder," another said.

"Life for a life," more began to repeat.

"What's happening?" Aden asked Kira as she knelt beside him.

She looked at Barra's body, his eyes still open. He had never showed her any kindness, and now he had sealed Aden's doom.

"The villagers' law," Kira said sadly. "Barra knew if he died by your hand, they would put you to death."

"And if he had killed me?" Aden interrupted, knowing the logic was flawed.

"He would have made an exception for himself," Kira replied, her mind spinning with what had just happened.

"Take his bow," Scelus, the lead guard, ordered as they pulled Aden to his feet, pushing Kira aside.

"I'll find a way. I'll talk to my father," Kira said confidently, pausing to look in Aden's confused eyes as her wings beat fiercely, lifting her away.

Rough hands yanked Aden's arms behind his back. Rope bit into his wrists, tied so tight his fingers went numb within minutes.

"Move," Scelus grunted.

As the villagers turned toward the path, the body of Barra lay on blood soaked grass.

"Should we bury him?" Malus, the second in command asked.

"He never said his preference...thought he would live forever." A villager replied.

"A warriors funeral then, let him become one with the beasts." Scelus announced as they took a moment to pick up his swords and left his body for the animals to consume.

Scelus knelt and closed Barra's eyes, letting his hand rest on Barra's chest for a moment. "Farewell old friend, we'll continue what you started."

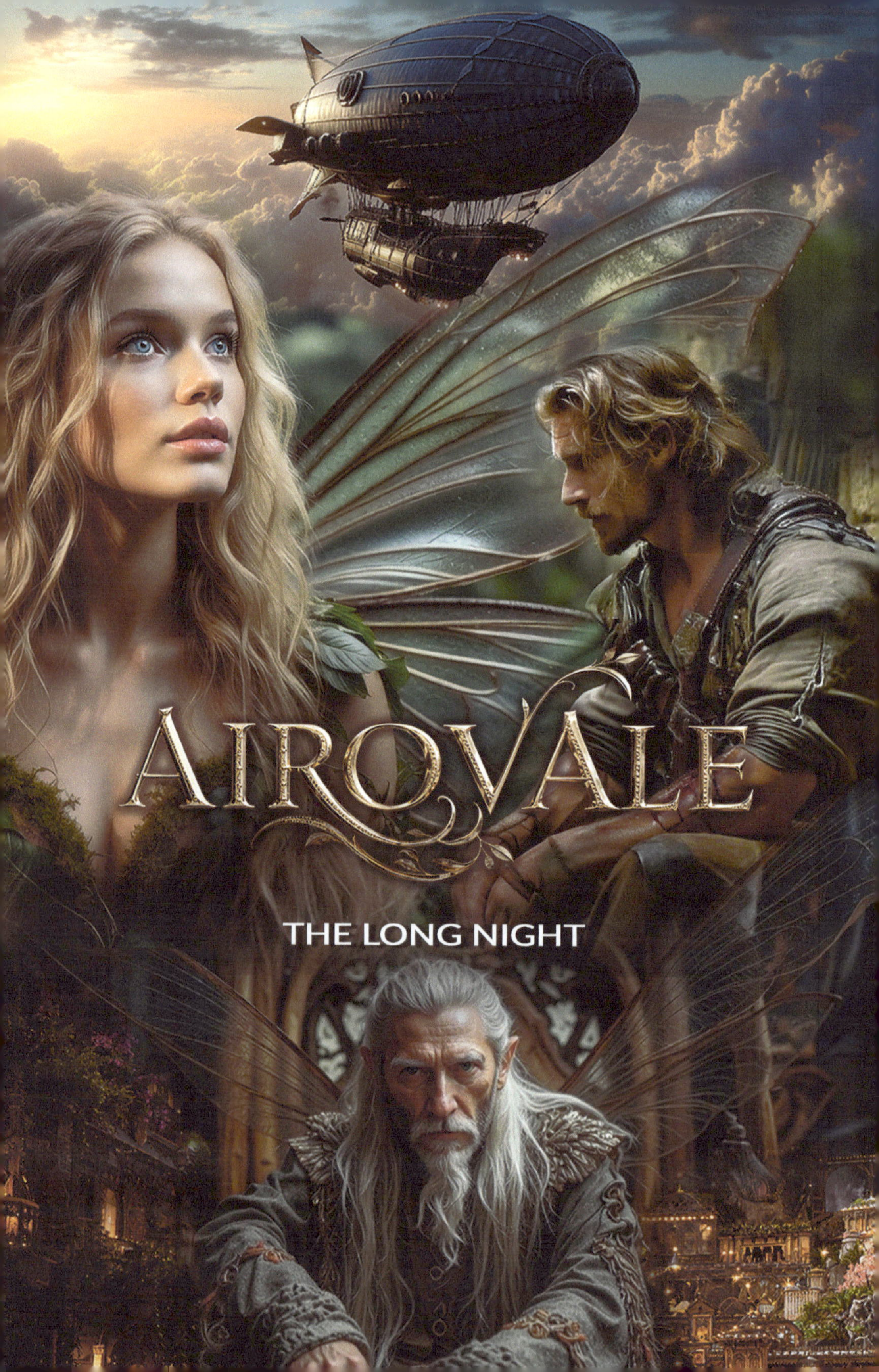

AIROVALE
THE LONG NIGHT

The Long Night

The Price of Greed

In the clouds above, the *Nereid* had pushed far enough into the western wind that Canyon Myst was no longer in view. They had enough treasure to build kingdoms, and just enough coal for the trip to the Crescent Islands, and then home to Airovale. Even if seven years had passed, all would be forgiven in the presence of their riches on return.

The crew speculated about the outcome of the duel. Even though Aden was a new face to them, he had taken great risks to warn them of the time paradox. But in considering their riches, their conscience was soothed to mild regret. The hull popped and creaked under the enormous weight of gold and gems as the crew shoveled coal to gain lift above the cloud line.

Von Holt's commands were relayed by Steffan into the boiler room. "More coal! Keep that box full!"

The crew obeyed, working nonstop to do the task previously accomplished by Aden.

Hours passed, elevations increased, and the *Nereid* found a tailwind to guide it farther west. Von Holt's compass spun uselessly, only affirming they were over the magnetic sea, their true direction unknown, under a sky with no stars.

Steffan went to the captain's cabin, where they sorted through maps that might indicate proximity to the Crescent Islands in the coming days. The captain knew his experience was the only navigation until land was spotted, and his apprehension was causing him to doubt if he had chosen the right course.

"Not a star to guide her by," Von Holt muttered under his breath, measuring distances between landmarks.

"We have a bigger problem," Steffan replied, motioning for the captain to follow him.

Von Holt followed Steffan to the boiler room, where a handful of crewmembers hovered around the boiler door, watching the coal burn.

"Show him," Steffan ordered as they opened a space for the captain to watch.

The man pulled the door open wide and thrust a shovel full of coal into the firebox, igniting it like paper in a flame, dissolving to ash instantly.

Von Holt's brow pressed down in disbelief as he leaned closer, watching the coal crumble from black to grey before his eyes. He had seen old coal before with a fraction of the expected potency, but nothing so ancient that it crumbled in the fire. He took a breath and asked his first mate the question everyone in the room already knew.

"How much do we have left?" he sighed, walking toward the hold, where coal was normally piled up to the roof for long trips.

No one answered; their greed and shame had already condemned them. Von Holt turned to the coal hold, loaded with gold stacked tightly into every corner, with only a small pile of coal left in front of it.

"This is all you gathered?" he erupted.

"It was full, sir, to the ceiling. We used it to get aloft," Steffan replied, knowing it made no difference now.

"What should have lasted weeks withered in hours," Von Holt announced, his voice sounding hollow. "Look at us, every man as rich as a king, floating out here in the forgotten blue."

He walked toward the door, patting Steffan on the shoulder, "You were right old friend."

Von Holt looked around the boiler room at the faces of the men, they were scared and had good reason to be. He turned without another word, and slammed the door behind him.

Moments later, he walked along the deck and stood at the gap in the rail, where the gangplank went down. The wind pulled at his coat. Below, the magnetic sea churned in darkness. He thought of his pride, not wanting to admit he had nothing to indicate where they were. A ship full of treasure that couldn't fuel the journey or feed the crew. The memory of reliving weeks in the clouds haunted him. Then he thought of his wife who was ill when he departed, the doctors he would pay on return, to make her well. Seven years gone, and the entire ship's fortune couldn't buy a single day. Not for her, for him, or the crew.

He took a breath, removed the safety rope, and stepped off the edge.

"Man overboard!" the night watchman shouted, rushing to reach the captain, but he had already fallen into the fog below.

The richest ship ever to rise into the skies had become a drifting tomb. Favoring gems over fuel, they drifted into the storm, where fate collected the balance due.

But Aden's fate was still being written.

Return to the Village

The path back to the village wound through forest, then open field. Aden stumbled on a root he couldn't see in the fading light. Without his hands to catch himself, he went down hard, face-first into the dirt. His shoulder took the impact, pain shooting through the joint.

He lay there a moment, tasting blood and soil.

"Get up," the guard said flatly.

Aden rolled to his knees, struggling to his feet. No one helped. They just watched, bored.

"Clumsy for an aeronaut," Malus mocked while the others laughed.

The ropes mixed with dirt and sweat cut into his wrists, as he tried to ignore the burning sensation of numbness in his arms.

The path turned into the jungle, as they walked in the dimming light of sunset. Fireflies began to appear, lighting the way. His mind went back to earlier in the day when he walked similar trails with Kira.

His thoughts replayed each moment, each discovery, and the incredible sensation of kissing her. When he blinked his eyes, he saw her face, and heard her voice. Hours passed in silence as he ignored the conversations of the guards, and thought only of the fairy that had captured his heart.

As they neared the village, faces appeared in doorways. Word of Barra's death spread at the speed of the footsteps ahead of them, villagers heard the news and looked toward Aden in judgment. Some watched with pity. Others looked away quickly, afraid to be seen sympathizing.

Malus pushed the villagers back as they began to press around them. Scelus walked ahead, clearing a path toward the jail, as a villager retold the events.

The entire village was in shock, knowing their laws, but also knowing Barra had caused his own demise.

Olga carried a bucket, pushing past the guards and villagers, annoyed by their gawking and whispers.

"Peet! Peet" She demanded as she walked to Aden and lifted a ladle of water to his chapped lips.

It spilled down his face as he tried to gulp as much as he could before she was pushed aside by the guards.

"You're wasting your time, Olga" Malus chided.

Olga took the ladle and struck Malus repeatedly in the face and chest, as she accused him of torture in her language—her words emphasized by each strike, until he stepped back and held up his hands in surrender.

She gave Aden another drink, then shook her head in sadness at what had happened. She then pointed to his wrists as he passed by, insisting they do something about his purple fingers.

Aden turned and made eye contact with Olga, nodding in gratitude for her defiant kindness.

She stood in the crowd, holding the ladle to her chest, full of sorrow over Barra's death, and the coming judgement of the young aeronaut.

By the time they reached the jail, the moon was over the canyon, and Aden could barely stand.

A young fairy watched from the trees above the canyon and flew way toward Sibhruion.

The Cell

A heavy wooden door opened, creaking at the hinges from rare use, as they motioned for Aden to step inside.

"Wait, let me cut the ropes." Malus said.

His knife swiped through the ropes, cutting into Aden's wrist without concern of pain or injury.

Aden felt his arms finally released, and held his wrists in his hands, wiping the dirt and blood away as the sensation of circulation surged to his fingers.

Scelus placed his boot on Aden's back and kicked him into the cell, then slammed the door.

Aden stumbled but kept his balance, relieved to be alone, as he looked around the dim room.

The high walled cell was constructed of stones from the river, with a floor hewn from jagged lava rock. A path was worn smooth across from the floor between the door and a bench that was fixed into the wall. It was the bed, chair and table for anyone doomed to sleep there. Aden sat and looked up at the ceiling. Small, barred windows near the top let the village lights seep in through the vapor of damp canyon air.

A bucket half filled with hay sat in the corner, flies circling.

A slot near the bottom of the door opened abruptly, followed by a tray of food that was pushed through without concern of how it landed, spilling everything across the floor.

"I'm not hungry." Aden said to himself, comparing the jail to the one at Airovale. It was quiet and free of rodents, compared to the place he had spent three months before becoming an aeronaut.

He sat on the bench and collapsed against the wall, rubbing circulation back into his hands. His fingers were stiff and swollen. The rope had left deep grooves in his skin.

Outside he could hear people in the streets, outburst of shock as one villager told another.

"Life for a life." Aden whispered, "I let that bastard live! He did this to himself!"

A Father's Wisdom

In Sibhruion, news of Barra's demise and the man who had killed him had already reached the fae village. The palace had been told Aden would be executed for the crime. Their sympathy for his defense, and distaste for Barra's treachery, drew sentiment, but the human elders insisted that their law be followed.

The fae cared little for human disputes, but how Aden knew of the time paradox on the island raised concerns among the fae leaders.

A crowd gathered at the entrance of the fae palace, demanding answers as Kira arrived, pushing through, her voice breaking as the fae elders discussed concerns over the pact. Faces turned toward her, some with sympathy, others hardened by the law of trespass in the ancient ruins.

"Ah there she is!" an elder mocked while pointing in her direction.

Thalos stepped to his throne as accusations flew, assumptions hardening before hearing the truth of the incident. Kira's emotions seethed with desperation and anger as she tried to correct every misspoken word of gossip.

Thalos knew she would only sound more guilty if she continued. He raised his hand, creating a crack of thunder in the room, which quieted the crowd instantly.

"We'll not be taking action on any trespass in the ruins today, unless those of you who have also snuck down there in the past are ready to confess your poor judgment," Thalos began.

The crowd's murmurs quieted as they stepped back from Kira, knowing many of them had mingled with humans at times, and made the same journey as Kira.

Kira saw her father handle the crowd with wise strength, but her heart was in terror for what would happen to Aden.

"They are going to execute him!" Kira pleaded. "He is innocent. Aden showed mercy, and Barra charged him, falling on his own sword!"

"And why was your betrothed fighting with a castaway?" Elgin, a fae elder, interjected, knowing the answer was incriminating.

"Enough!" Thalos commanded. "None of us are shedding tears over Barra, especially you, Elgin."

Elgin lifted his face to the crowd, "I admit, I mocked him for the pompous boar that he was. Always scheming and intimidating his people. But they chose him as their leader, and their leader maintains the pact!"

The crowd responded in agreement, nodding their heads as Elgin continued.

"Did you think of that, when you dishonored us by calling the beasts, or taking a human below the forbidden river?" Elgin prodded as he pointed his hand toward Kira.

Thalos felt a rage come over him, "No one honors the pact more than a father giving his daughter to keep an alliance," Thalos said, walking in contempt toward Elgin. "You can lecture us on honor when you admit your daughter fled the island, WITH your blessing, leaving me to give Kira in her place!" Thalos shouted.

Elgin nodded and backed away in humility, remembering he begged Thalos not to punish him when his daughter boarded a ship in the night to escape her fate as the future wife of Barra.

The crowd responded, giving their respect to Thalos, as the wisest.

"The humans will elect a new leader and solve their own problems. This is my judgment," Thalos said with iron authority.

The crowd nodded and whispered as they began exiting the palace.

Kira moved to her father's throne, kneeling beside him.

"Please! Can't you talk to the human elders? You don't know what it's like to face death!" Kira cried, her voice carrying through the palace. "He was only defending himself; I have to save him!"

Gasps rippled through the onlookers, but Thalos reached for her and held her tightly. He drew her away from the others, closing the palace doors. There, away from prying eyes, his ancient voice broke as the memories poured forth.

"My daughter, I do know what it's like to face death," he said.

"I've not told you the entire story of the ancient world. I was not born after the great eruption...I was there when the mountain woke and poured fire over the city. We were all doomed. Some took to the sea, but there were not enough ships. Some flew until their wings gave out and they fell into the ocean. We fled to the temple, where time moves like the tide. For a moment, a passage opened and we stepped through, carried into tomorrow. We arrived here many generations ago, our city buried under the river. We barely survived the journey to the surface."

Kira's face flushed. All those years of patience, of quiet counsel—it made sense now. He was compelled to give her as a wife to maintain the human pact, but his generations had shown him that real love ruled over duty.

"This means you are many more generations than everyone thinks!" Kira realized.

"Thank you for noticing." Thalos joked as Kira felt his familiar wit lighten the moment.

"How do you always know how to make me laugh when I'm upset?" She asked, remembering the familiarity of the moment with Aden.

"Ah, you're just like your mother. Locked in a room of emotions, waiting for someone to open the door with a laugh to let you out." He replied, seeing his wife in Kira's face.

"There's a way to save him, Kira," he said gently. "It would save you both, but it would mean an eternal farewell if you take it. My time draws near, soon. I've already seen it. We part now, or we part later. But I would rather know you made a life with a good man you loved, than whomever the humans choose next to lead them."

"Couldn't I bring him here to live with us?" Kira asked, hoping for a compromise that spared her beloved and kept her father nearby.

"If only it were so easy." Thalos said as he held his daughter's hand in his.

"They will hunt you both, with equal penalty. Once you free Aden, you will be charged as if you killed Barra as well, some are already suggesting it. There is no safety here from that moment. Only time can save you," Thalos whispered, keeping their conversation private.

Kira held her father, realizing he proposed a choice that meant never seeing her again.

"You remind me so much of your mother, ready to sacrifice everything for the one you love." Thalos said as he held her close and fought the tears that memories brought.

"I don't know what to do. Where should we go?" Kira asked, as she wiped her eyes.

"You've already found where, now we need to find when." Thalos said as he guided her toward the library, "Imagine a journey that can only be taken once..."

The Long Night

Hours passed. The light from the window faded to the glow of a half moon. The village was silent, taverns closed in mourning for their lost leader. Crickets pulsed a sound that echoed through the canyon as footsteps of the pacing guards could be heard outside.

The men standing watch over the jail gathered by the high window for a drink of water, unaware the sound carried up through the opening.

"D'you get that from Olga?" Scelus jeered.

"Very funny." Malus held the bucket and sipped from the ladle. "In the morning then?"

"First light. I requested that we use Barra's sword but they insisted on the cliffs." Scelus replied.

"Why not both?" Another guard joined, "Sword...then over the side."

"It's not up to us, the elders decide." Scelus said sternly, "For now."

"Is that still...possible" a fourth guard asked, looking around to ensure secrecy.

"The Exile seems to think so, we'll pick a new leader, have the wedding, and continue with the plan."

Aden listened, unsure of their conclusions, but worried that Kira may not have been spared from a life unwillingly betrothed. Their mention of cliffs stayed in his mind, perhaps a fall to his death, perhaps another unarmed battle.

Now he was assured, this was his last night alive. He worried for Kira's safety, had she spoken to her father, was she in danger, was there anything Thalos could do?

He thought of her wings, her laughter, the way she'd looked at him in the waterfall's mist. She'd spent centuries being someone's tool, someone's duty, someone's key to power.

Just once, let me choose, she'd said.

She'd chosen him. And tomorrow they'd kill him for it.

His hand went to his neck, touching his goggles and wondering if this was why his father never returned. Had he met a similar fate of unexpected circumstances that cost him his life, or trapped him by choice?

The stars wheeled slowly overhead. He didn't sleep.

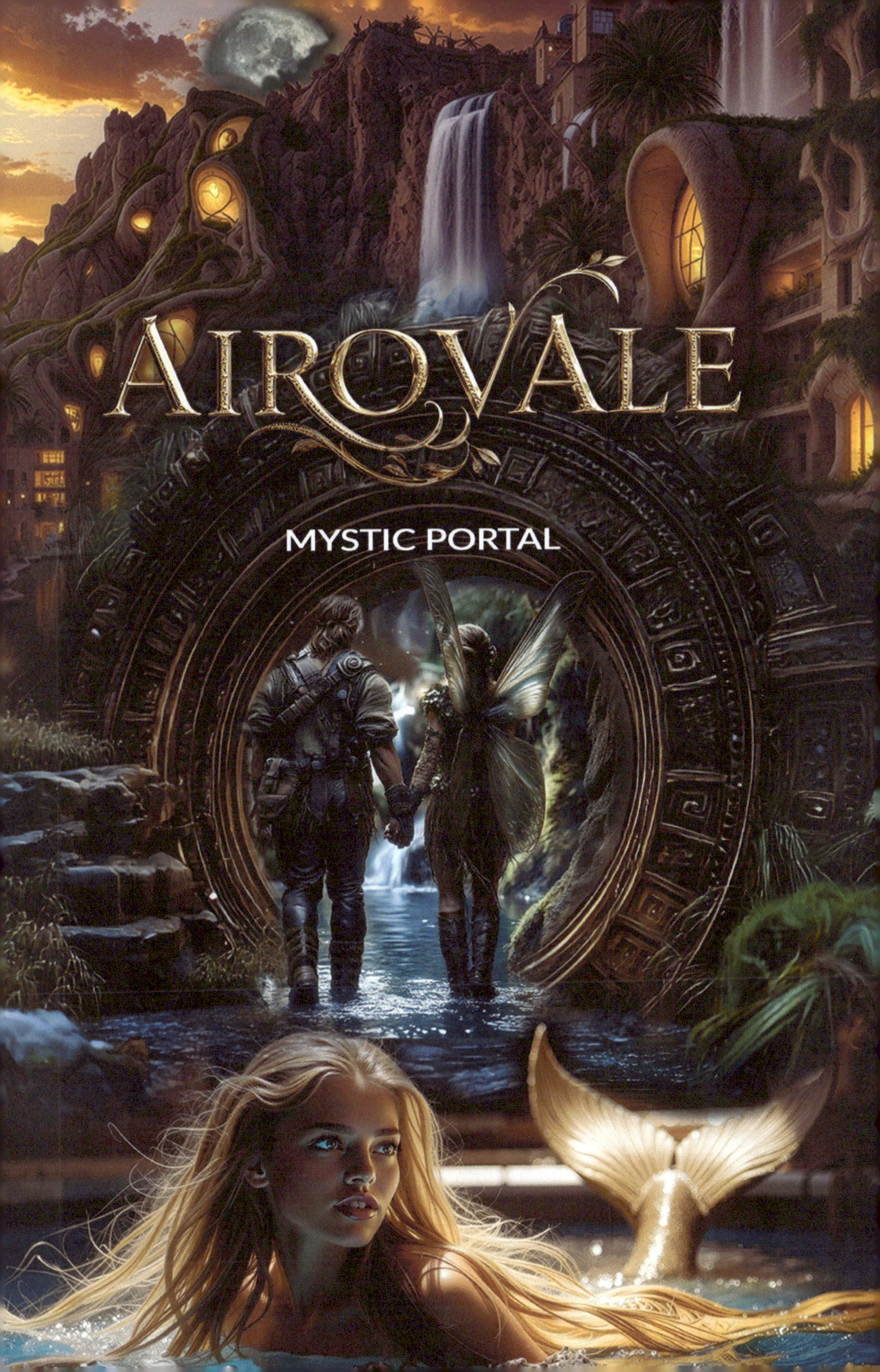
AIROVALE
MYSTIC PORTAL

Mystic Portal

The Rescue

That same night, she flew under the fog into the jungle near the village, landing at the ritual grounds, where her lifelong friends played in the waterfall. The Fae Guardian welcomed her, setting the fog to hide their presence. Kira shared her story, confessing her love for Aden. Her friend's eyes grew wide in amazement. Fairies loved for a lifetime; it was rare to be so confident in such a short time, but all were relieved that Barra was no longer her destiny.

Tears poured down Kira's face as she explained her plan. "I need to free him tonight and make our escape to the forbidden river. But the jail is heavily guarded."

The Fae Guardian began to smile, delighted with the excitement of saving her friend.

"We could make an early wedding present for you," she intimated, making eye contact with the other fairies.

Moments later, Kira walked through the narrow alley behind the prison. She looked back to the tall trees around the canyon, where a sparkle of light flashed.

"Did you see that?" Scelus asked, as he and three others on the street looked toward the treeline.

"It was something just there," he said, pointing at the trees, as Kira slipped to the prison door behind them.

She pressed herself against the prison wall. Her hand trembled as she reached toward the iron lock.

She knew what it would cost. Iron didn't just burn fae—it seared like acid, ate through skin until it found bone. But she'd made her choice already.

Her trembling fingertip touched the metal.

White-hot agony lanced through her hand. She clamped her other hand over her mouth, teeth digging into her palm to keep from screaming. Tears streamed down her face as fae magic poured from her burning finger into the lock's seams.

The metal hissed where her skin touched it. The smell of burning flesh rose in the air.

The bar snapped free with a dull thud.

Kira jerked her hand back, cradling it against her chest. Her fingertip was blistered, the skin swelling as the pain persisted. She pressed her lips together, breathing hard through her nose, willing herself not to make a sound.

The guards were still looking at the trees.

She slipped inside, pulling the door closed behind her.

Aden's eyes widened as the door creaked. "Kira...?" he whispered.

Then he saw her hand—the fingertip pale white, already blistering beneath the skin. She held it against her chest, trembling.

"Come," she gasped. "We don't have much time."

The courtyard stirred with shouts. The guards reacted to a pack of tigers, roaming the streets near the jail. Their growls echoed deeply off the canyon walls as each tiger chose a guard to pursue.

Still cradling her burned hand, Kira reached for Aden with the other, pulling him toward the door.

"Get ready to run!" she whispered.

Aden tightened his bootstraps and brushed his hair from his eyes. "Ready."

The door opened to the chaos of four tigers, a performance of pursuit, chasing men they could have eaten by surprise had they wished.

Kira and Aden slipped into the alley and ran for the jungle as her friends passed them on their way into the village.

Aden had never seen so many fae before; their glowing faces and mischievous giggles washed over him as he and Kira faded into the dark.

"Who were they?" he asked as they ran down the path from the village.

"My friends. Keep running," she replied, trying to stay beside him without flying.

The villagers began to stir, lighting torches and running through the streets to help the guards. Hunting weapons and bows appeared, making the scene too dangerous for the fae.

"Apologies, dear people!" the Fae Guardian announced loudly, motioning for the tigers to join the other fairies.

"They are like children sometimes, playing a game, but they would never have harmed you," she said, as each fairy came and walked away with their companion.

The fairies mimed an enchantment spell, softening the guards' resolve to fight.

"No problem!" Scelus announced, puffing his chest to impress the Guardian.

"False alarm, everyone. No harm done," he dismissed, as the other guards agreed and climbed down from trees and out from under crates.

Each man nodded and smiled as the fairies left the village, their soft laughter mixed with obedient tigers' growls.

Malus wiped the dust from his clothing and walked back toward the jail.

"Did you see how she looked at me?" he asked the other guards.

They arrived at the jail, where the broken lock had left the door hanging partially open. Moments later, the guards raised the alarm, lighting torches as they headed into the woods. Those loyal to Barra gave chase, intending to execute upon capture.

Through the Veil

Aden and Kira fled into the night, pursued through the forest, the echo of voices swelling behind them. Torches flared in the dark, men shouting threats as they closed the distance. Branches snapped, feet pounded, every step a race against judgment.

Finally, they reached the forbidden forest, stumbling into the stream, water rushing at their waists. Kira submerged her burned hand in the current, gasping softly at the cold relief, before reaching for Aden with the other.

Their warm embrace melted the shivers caused by the river's cold. Their hearts beat like drums as Aden held Kira tightly, wading them into deeper water to conceal their location. She kept her arms around him, catching her breath, as he pushed them farther out until his feet could no longer touch the bottom.

With a shimmer, they took a breath and kissed as the bubble enveloped them, carrying them beneath, while shouts thundered helplessly above. No one could follow. Only the caves and currents knew their escape.

They drifted swiftly, the current pulling them through a luminous channel until the river widened, revealing the cavern temple. Mist coiled across the floor, and the glyphs on the wall glowed as if they had been waiting for them.

Aden pressed his hand against the stone where he had before. Mist rose, but the tunnel passage did not open.

Kira ran her fingers across the images carved in stone: suns, the mountain, cities, and an island. "They've changed," she breathed. "The order tells a different story now."

Aden stepped back, staring at the entire cave wall, piecing the sequence together. The subtle details of each carving were not duplicates; they were different events. The sun was positioned differently compared to the island, the city was above the water or below it, and the mountain was whole or broken into parts.

"This is the history of the island," Aden said confidently.

"Occurring in any order," Kira replied, understanding more after Thalos explained the portal.

They examined each detail. "I think the city below the water is…now?" Aden said.

Kira looked closely, repeating her father's words, "Each glyph maps to an epoch of time, matching the ones around the tunnel entrance."

Kira touched the stone carved in the shape of the sun rising over the whole mountain.

"This was centuries before the eruption," she said, as the carvings pulsed with light. An ominous hum vibrated the walls as fog poured from the mouth of the tunnel.

"A path to another time…is it possible?" Aden asked in shock.

"My father came through it to escape the great eruption; that's the symbol there." She pointed at a glyph where sun hovered over the mountain as it split.

Tears welled in her eyes, as she felt the sadness of saying goodbye to him.

"Maybe he can come back after us and join us there?" Aden said, trying to comfort her while overwhelmed with the concept.

"No, it's not possible. He can't go through again, and we can never come back. It's one way only," Kira explained while wiping her tears away.

Aden gripped her hand. He reflected on his life, always on the outside, alone and struggling. It made sense now: nothing bound him there; the way forward was back in time.

"I'm ready," he said, though he had no idea what lay ahead.

Kira hesitated. She saw Barra's fury, her people's judgment, the centuries of duty that bound her. And yet she also saw Aden, the risk she had taken, the love that had awoken in her, the freedom she had never dared claim. One day beside him outweighed centuries without. Even her father had seen it and guided her to this moment. Aden was no longer a stranger. He was her future, and she was his.

Their fingers intertwined as they stepped into the waist-deep water and the fog from the tunnel grew heavier. The glyph of the unbroken mountain began to glow at the portal's edge, faint at first, then brighter as the chamber trembled.

"What do we do?" Aden asked.

"Hold on to me," Kira sighed, trembling in fear.

The water's current swept them inside as they embraced, plunging into darkness. Standing changed to floating in a pressure that wasn't wet but thick, like swimming through honey made of light.

Aden's stomach lurched. The sensation reminded him of falling, except they weren't falling—they were moving, pulled by something older than gravity. He tightened his arms around Kira as the darkness gave way to streaks of color, smeared and rushing past like arrows on fire.

"Don't let go," Kira breathed against his neck.

He couldn't have if he'd wanted to.

The world outside the tunnel blurred into motion. Days compressed into heartbeats. He saw the sun arc across the sky, again and again, a strobing rhythm that made his eyes ache. Seasons bled together—green to gold to white to green—flickering so fast they became a single muddy glow. The island above them shifted and breathed, trees growing and falling, storms sweeping through like ghosts.

Aden's chest tightened. He remembered being small in Airovale, maybe four or five, gripping the painted pole of a carousel horse while the world spun around him. His mother holding him in place, as the sensation of spinning took over. He'd felt terrified and thrilled, desperate to hold on, certain that if he let go, he'd fly away.

This was the same. Except there was no painted horse beneath him. Only Kira, whispering in his ear.

"I've got you," he said again, though the words came out strange, stretched thin by whatever force carried them.

The blur began to slow.

Colors sharpened. The strobing sun steadied into a single afternoon, golden light filtering through the cave mouth above them. Aden saw figures moving near the portal's edge—Mystics, fae and humans wearing simpler clothing than what he'd seen, their faces tight with purpose, as they carried belongings toward Aden and Kira.

Aden reached out and felt a barrier between them. Light came through but sound remained on the other side. "What is happening? Is this where we're going?"

Kira looked closely at the fairy in the crowd. It was Elgin's daughter, holding hands with a villager whose back was to them.

"So much for a ship in the night! That's Vivian! And... Barra's family?" She leaned closer to the barrier. "We were told they departed by ship!"

"How long ago was that?" Aden asked, studying the details around them.

"It was a generation ago, and... is that his brother?" Her mouth hung open. "Wait—why would they lie about leaving the island by ship?"

The illuminated glyph on the portal entrance was different than the one they had chosen. Aden looked at the order of them and saw it was in place along the edge, just before theirs.

"I think this is a memory that we're seeing," Aden said, while Kira shook her head at the scandal it would have been if Barra's brother had become the leader instead.

She looked into Aden's eyes. "I'm sorry, you're so serious and I'm acting like a gossiping adolescent. Yes, it's a memory, but who does it belong to?"

"It's not ours—we were never here," Aden replied, observing each detail of the cave.

"Maybe the portal remembers each time it was used?" Kira asked.

Aden nodded. "Then who makes the glyphs?"

The current pulled them onward back into the blur, faster now, years compressing into seconds. He felt Kira trembling against him, her wings encircling him, her heartbeat drumming against his chest in the dark.

They began to slow as the darkness peeled back into fire. Lava re-treated up the mountain, ash lifted from the streets, collapsed buildings reassembled stone by stone—time rewinding to the moment before catastrophe.

Then the memory began.

Aden saw a figure with wings—younger, darker-haired, but unmistakably Thalos—pressing the crowd inside, shouting commands. Fae and humans alike rushed toward the temple, toward the water, toward the only escape left.

"My father! Look how handsome he was!" Kira pressed her hand against the energy holding them inside.

Thalos grabbed a child from a collapsing archway and thrust her toward the portal. Then another. Then another. His face was streaked with soot and tears, his wings singed at the edges, but he didn't stop. He stood at the threshold of the tunnel and pushed survivor after survivor through, even as the lava crept closer.

"He saved so many," Kira breathed, her voice breaking.

Aden watched the young chief work until the last possible moment, until the fire licked at his heels, until he finally turned and ran toward a fairy waiting at the entrance for him. They embraced and jumped through as the lava swept over the scene.

"Was that... you?" Aden began.

"It was my mother. He always said I looked like her, but I didn't realize she came through with him." She sighed.

The scene dimmed for a moment, then light began to appear seconds later.

"What happened? Why are we still here?" Aden asked, looking at the unchanged glyphs.

"Is it a different time? Before the great eruption? Days, or—" Kira's words trailed off as the brightness of the portal began to shine, revealing the temple as it had been days before the lava ever touched it.

Polished marble walls, inlaid with golden filigree, lined toward staircases where a great pool glowed below them. The glyphs were freshly carved, the water crystal clear. An entire level of the great temple was revealed.

A lone figure appeared in the sparkling water, swimming to the edge and pausing, then stepping out to ascend the steps. They watched in amazement—a mermaid, transforming into a woman as she climbed the stairs.

"Is that—?" Aden asked.

"Sea Fae. I forgot they existed during this time. Their world would be destroyed by the lava flows."

"The city below the water, on the glyph!" Aden realized aloud.

Kira admired the mermaid's appearance. "She is beautiful. Look at that long hair."

"I'm... looking." Aden nodded.

Kira jabbed him with her elbow.

Aden glanced at her, smiling as he took her hand in his. The smile faded as a man entered the portal and walked toward the woman, embracing her.

He pointed excitedly at a cart of gold bars he had pulled with him. As he gestured to the portal and water below, she stepped back.

"Is that her... husband?" Aden asked.

"No, sea fae can only have children with their own kind." Kira watched the woman's posture. "She's afraid of him—look how she stands, arms crossed."

The man knelt at the water's edge, describing a plan, as the mermaid walked away. He looked up, realizing she had gone without a word.

"I know that look... obsession," Kira said. "That's how Barra used to look at me before I was promised to him."

"His ears... he's fae!" Aden said, catching a glimpse as the man's long hair shifted while he bent to lay gold on the ground. "But no wings?"

Kira stiffened in Aden's arms. "That's not possible—"

The current began to push them, accelerating before they could learn more, pulling them past the kneeling figure, past the gold, past the moment that might reveal the events leading up to the great eruption.

Once again, the sky lit like ribbons in the trail of the sun, as colors blurred around them.

Kira remembered spinning in place as a child, watching the fireflies begin as dots and stretch into streaks as she tried to go faster before collapsing in dizziness.

Then the lights slowed, the hum of moving through time faded, as sound returned—birdsong, wind, the gentle rush of water.

Aden felt ground beneath his feet. Solid. Real. He stood carefully, guiding Kira up beside him, both of them ankle-deep in a clear stream beneath arches of white stone and the unfinished carvings that would become the portal.

They had stopped.

Arrival

Blue domes gleamed under sunlight. Fountains splashed in distant courtyards. The air smelled of salt and flowers, and somewhere nearby, a child laughed.

Aden turned slowly, taking in the city around them. Fae and humans walked together along wide promenades, their clothing bright, their faces untroubled. Market stalls lined the waterfront. Music drifted from an open window.

On the horizon, the mountain stood whole and quiet, a thin ribbon of smoke curling from its peak—a warning no one here would heed for centuries.

Kira wrapped her hands around his arm, holding tightly.

"We made it," he said softly. Then, quieter: "Now, we decide what happens next."

Kira looked at him, her eyes still wet, and something in her expression shifted. Not grief. Gratitude.

They had left behind a world that no longer fit them, taking no map, gold, or plan—only each other, and the knowledge that sharing the path was enough.

The mountain whispered smoke on the horizon.

But that reckoning was centuries away.

Today, the sun was warm, and they were free.

■■■

Epilogue

The Exchange of Time: An Author's Reflection on *Airovale*

Airovale is more than a story about zeppelins, faeries, and enchanted islands. On the surface, it tells of lost aeronauts stumbling into a world where time flows differently, of Mystics who live by laws no outsider fully understands. But beneath the myths, it is a tale of choices; what we pursue, what we sacrifice, and the exchanges we make without always realizing the cost.

The project began as a single short video reel for my social media channels: a zeppelin drifting into a steampunk port, a medieval village, and some engaging characters. It took weeks to learn how to make the first micro-film, mixing my graphic skills with assistance from AI programs for scene design and animation. Finally, there it was, a video series called *Airovale* named as a nod to AI for helping me draw the characters. The story, however, had been forming from years of reflection, metaphor with a hidden truth.

The Quartermaster's Lesson

The old quartermaster embodies that hidden truth. No longer chasing adventure, he sits quietly at the edge of the village, pipe in hand, and sees what others cannot: we are already rich.

But we live as though we are not. We trade gratitude for desire, chasing the next horizon, the next treasure, the next victory. Only later do we realize that what we abandoned in the name of success:

friendships, laughter, time with our beloved; were the treasures we sought all along.

The Law of Exchange

The *Canyon Myst* island reveals a law the faeries know well: nothing is gained without something given in return. The Mystics guard this law; the crew of the *Nereid* resist it. They want more without losing anything, as we all so often do. At first they wanted a place to land, food, and a way home to *Airovale.*

But, once inside the volcano's mines, they looked past the coal and gathered gems instead. All they needed was fuel to get home but to return as wealthy men was more appealing. What they didn't see was that time itself was the price. A day on *Canyon Myst* was a year in *Airovale.* By the time, they could have returned, their children would be grown, and their families would have assumed them for dead. Making the time lost more valuable than any amount of riches.

This is not just a plot twist. Every choice we make trades something: work for family time, ambition for rest, comfort for risk. Every 'yes' is also a 'no'. We cannot escape the law of exchange.

Kira and Aden

At the center is the fragile bond between Kira, a faerie, and Aden, a crewman. To choose each other is to betray their worlds. Kira is bound to the Mystics' duty; Aden belongs to a world of conquest and consumption. Their love makes sense to the heart, but not to the life each must return to. Yet, they connect in a way that assures them, they will succeed together without knowing how.

We're not meant to have so many assurances, and the story gives hints about that. The map, the riches, duty, time, all set aside for what happens in the heart. We all know this struggle. To commit to one path is to close others. Their story reflects our own—where loyalty, longing, and sacrifice collide. We choose who we share our path with, and that is enough.

Time as Treasure

The deepest current in *Airovale* is time itself. On the island of *Canyon Myst*, to stay is to forfeit the future; to leave is to abandon the present. The villagers who had remained there understood their families had passed on hundreds of years ago, leaving them with fading memories that dulled the meaning of life, until emptiness was all that remained.

So, it is with us. We often spend time as though it were endless, only to discover too late that it was the most precious and irreplaceable treasure. Hours with children, talks with parents, laughter with friends, these cannot be reclaimed once traded away. Time is priceless.

Why I Wrote *Airovale*

The characters portrayed in the first four *Airovale* videos were captured while living a simple life, requiring no explanation or language to understand the scenes. This is especially true in episode 4, *Coming Home*—my personal favorite in the entire set of microfilms. Chapter 4 features a village as the airships are returning, families gather and what matters most is measured.

As I was creating episode four, it occurred to me that the visual message was more than the obvious. There was a backstory, a depth to each movement, each smile. And that became *Airovale*. A written journey of the characters, expanding the significance and meaning of every scene.

I compared lessons from my own life and found myself thinking like the quartermaster—weighing the choices and the cost.

Fantasy became philosophy. Escapism became reflection. *Airovale* was not about another world; it was about the exchanges that shapes ours. Awakening to the idea that even if you achieve everything you ever wanted, you cannot anticipate how you will feel when you have it. Happiness isn't an island where we arrive after a journey. Happiness is the journey, who we travel with, and how we anticipate coming home.

Gratitude as the Final Exchange

In the end, gratitude becomes the truest choice. Not sentiment, but action—the decision to see what we already have as enough, to live richly in the present instead of postponing joy for tomorrow. Gratitude turns fleeting time into lasting memory.

This sounds simple, but we're not born grateful. We learn it from parents at first, and later through loss or choices that ended in regret. It seems we wish for more, and once that wish in our hand, a new desire appears without appreciating the gain—robbed of the intended fulfillment, desire awakens to set a new goal. This theme was contrasted by the heroic actions aboard the *Ironnwind*, and the greed aboard the *Nereid and Gilded Star*.

That is the takeaway of *Airovale*: that by observing the choices of the characters, readers might recognize their own path and make a course correction. Not to see choices as burdens, but as the very fabric of a grateful life. And to consider how much we have been given before blindly seeking more.

Closing

Thank you for taking this journey with me. What began as an Instagram reel, grew into a series of videos, and became this book. My gratitude to you as a reader, is also an invitation: enter *Airovale* as a traveler. Let the choices of the crew, faeries, and Mystics guide you—while considering your own path.

Because if the quartermaster is right—and I believe he is—we are already rich. The challenge is simply to live as though we are.

Connect

Connect with the author for information on the next episode of Airovale (Summer 2026), enhanced content, including the Airovale cinematic films and soundtrack at:

www.Airovale.com

All primary social channels: @airovale

Lore of Airovale

A Guide to the Southern Sea and Its Mysteries

Geography of the Southern Sea

The Southern Sea stretches vast and treacherous between the mainland and the archipelagos beyond. At its heart lies **Airovale**, the capital city of aeronautics—a bustling port where zeppelins are forged and fortunes are made. Stone towers overlook the docks, quartermaster ledgers track every vessel, and the ceremonial bells ring for each homecoming. Beyond Airovale's shores, the sea transforms.

The Magnetic Sea begins where compasses spin uselessly and blue lightning cracks through cloudless skies. Aeronauts call this passage **Aelmir's Span**, named for the storm-bearded giant whose winds can turn a ship inside out. Navigation here requires experience, instinct, and no small measure of luck. Some ships turn back. Others press forward, gambling on the promise of copper and gold.

The Crescent Islands rise from the sea like volcanic teeth—canyons shrouded in perpetual fog, rivers carving deeper each season, and caves rich with copper ore. Markets cling to cliff terraces where farmers grow what they can. But the Crescents are best known for what lies hidden: a temple filled with gold, guarded by ancient magic and a witch's curse.

Canyon Myst exists on no official map. It is a place between myth and matter, where time moves differently and two peoples—human and fae—coexist under a fragile pact. One day spent on its shores costs a year beyond. The island never gives; there is only exchange.

Beneath Canyon Myst's river lies the **Ancient City**, drowned centuries ago when the great volcano woke. Its ruins hold secrets older than memory—glyphs that sing of time's flow, portals that bridge past and present, and the remnants of a civilization that learned too late what it meant to bargain with forces beyond comprehension.

The Law of Exchange

Magic on Canyon Myst operates by one immutable principle: **The island never gives—there is only exchange.**

Every gift demands payment. Every act of taking incurs a cost.

The Time Paradox is the island's most brutal exchange. For every day spent on Canyon Myst, a year passes in the world beyond. Aeronauts who linger too long return to find their children grown, their spouses aged or buried, their lives transformed by decades lost. The fae use this knowledge to encourage swift departures; humans who overstay their welcome pay the price in stolen time.

The Temple Gold carries its own curse. Guarded by Mahala, the gold is not hidden but offered—piled in ceremonial rings around pools of molten rock. To take it is to trigger the storm. To possess it is to invite ruin. The gold always returns, carried back by tide and wreckage, to wait for the next fool bold enough to claim it.

The **Portal Beneath the River** is the island's most mysterious exchange. Glyphs carved into stone depict the island's history across epochs—the mountain whole, the mountain broken, the city above water, the city drowned. Each glyph is a door. To choose one is to step through time itself, trading the present for the past, the known for the unknown. Those who pass through can never return.

Fae Magic and Culture

The fae of Canyon Myst are creatures of air and earth, ancient beyond measure, bound to the island by forces older than the pact.

Fae Magic manifests in many forms:

- **Wings of light** allow flight and swift passage through dense jungle
- **Bond with beasts**—tigers especially—grants protection and companionship

- **Enchanted bubbles** form underwater, allowing fae to travel submerged rivers and caves

- **Glamours and illusions** soften mortal resolve, turning aggression to bewilderment

- **Time-sense**—a subtle awareness of temporal flow and paradox

The **Fae Guardian** is both title and role—a position of trust within the fae community, responsible for maintaining sacred sites and mediating between fae and human settlements. Guardians are often the first to welcome or warn visitors, their presence a reminder that Canyon Myst is not undefended.

Sibhruion is the hidden palace of the fae, nestled deep within the island's heart. Its halls are carved from living stone, its throne room lit by phosphorescent moss. Here, Thalos presides over his people with wisdom born of centuries and sorrow earned through loss.

The **Pact** between fae and humans is maintained through marriage and mutual respect. Human leaders offer daughters to fae elders; fae offer protection and guidance in return. It is an uneasy peace, tested by pride and strained by cultural differences, but it has endured for generations.

Mythology: Aelmir, Mahala, and the Curse

Aelmir is the storm itself—a force of nature personified, described in legend as a bearded giant who walks across clouds. He does not answer to mortals, but to those with power enough to summon him. His winds are deliberate, his lightning precise. To cross Aelmir's Span is to risk his attention, and few who draw his gaze survive unscathed.

Mahala and Malina were once ordinary women—twin sisters, farmers' daughters, living in the shadow of the great volcano. When the mountain woke and poured fire through their valley, Mahala was burned beyond recognition, her body scarred from head to toe.

Malina saved her sister but could not heal her suffering. In desperation, Mahala prayed to the darkness for beauty restored and revenge against the sister whose pity cut deeper than the burns. The darkness answered, as it always does, but magic bound by blood is never precise.

Both sisters were granted eternal youth. Mahala's beauty returned, flawless and unchanging. But the cost was steep: she could never leave the island, bound forever as guardian of the temple gold. If the gold is taken, her scars return, and the years she has lived collapse upon her all at once.

Malina, untouched by flame but forever altered by the curse, fled the island in the arms of an aeronaut. She lives on, ageless and sorrowful, carrying the weight of centuries and the guilt of survival. The map she passes to explorers is both mercy and cruelty—a chance to end her sister's imprisonment, or a trap that leads only to ruin.

The storm Mahala summons is Aelmir's wrath unleashed. When thieves take what was offered in exchange, she draws symbols in wet sand and calls the giant to bring them down. The sea returns the gold; it always does.

The Culture of Aeronauts

To fly is to live. This is the creed of Airovale.

Aeronauts are more than pilots; they are heroes, adventurers, and gamblers all at once. They wear **goggles** as symbols of their trade—leather-strapped and brass-rimmed, pushed up on foreheads during rest, pulled down during flight. When the tower bells ring a homecoming, families don goggles in solidarity, a gesture of respect and shared identity.

Zeppelins are the lifeblood of commerce and culture. Built from iron ribs and canvas, fueled by coal and steam, these vessels carry copper from distant mines, trade goods across the sea, and aeronauts toward fortune or folly. Each ship has a name, a history, and a captain whose reputation determines whether crews sign on or turn away.

The **voyage to the Crescents** is both opportunity and ordeal. Officially, ships go for copper. In truth, every crew dreams of finding the temple gold. The journey takes two weeks across the Magnetic Sea, where compasses fail and navigation becomes an art. Those who return are celebrated; those who don't are mourned, their names added to ledgers kept in the quartermaster's tower.

"Na Dobro"—a phrase borrowed from the traders of the eastern steppes—means "for good" or "for the best." It is spoken as blessing and benediction, a recognition that kindness carries unseen weight and every gift sets something in motion.

Glossary of Terms

Aeronaut – Pilot or crew member of an airship; cultural hero in Airovale

Aelmir – Storm god of the Southern Sea, summoned by Mahala

Aelmir's Span – The passage across the Magnetic Sea where compasses fail

Airovale – Capital city of aeronautics, home port for zeppelin fleets

Canyon Myst – Hidden island where time moves differently; one day = one year beyond

Crescent Islands – Volcanic archipelago known for copper mines and temple gold

Fae Guardian – Title for fae responsible for sacred sites and mediation

Law of Exchange – The principle governing Canyon Myst: the island never gives, only exchanges

Magnetic Sea – Body of water where magnetic forces disrupt navigation

Na Dobro – "For good" (Ukrainian); blessing spoken with gifts or kindness

Sibhruion – Hidden palace of the fae, throne of Thalos

The Ancient City – Drowned civilization beneath Canyon Myst's river

The Pact – Alliance between fae and humans, maintained through marriage

Time Paradox – One day on Canyon Myst equals one year in the outside world

A Note on Maps

The map included in this volume depicts the Southern Sea and its surrounding territories as understood by the cartographers of Airovale. Canyon Myst does not appear on any official chart—its location is known only to those who have been there and survived to speak of it. The Ancient City exists in memory and ruin, accessible only through means best left undiscovered by the unwary.

Time is the only treasure. Spend it wisely.

Dramatis Personae

The Characters of Airovale

◈ **WARNING: This section contains spoilers for major plot events, character fates, and story outcomes. Recommend reading only after completing the book.**

Primary Characters

Aden — Gaunt young man, orphaned and once jailed for stealing, joins the *Nereid* as crew. Struggles with survival vs. belonging; becomes central in discovering the time-exchange truth and Kira's companion. His hunger for more than survival makes him reckless, but also empathetic to others cast aside. Aden's choices become the moral pivot of the tale, showing how love can outweigh treasure or duty. An outsider who finally finds a place to belong—even if it exists centuries in the past.

Kira — Daughter of Thalos, fae with rebellious heart, falls in love with Aden despite her arranged betrothal to Barra. Helps him uncover the secrets of the ancient city and ultimately escapes with him through time. Her defiance of duty for love marks the turning point of the saga. Kira bridges two worlds, embodying both the burden of tradition and the courage to choose differently. In her, we see that even immortals must sometimes choose mortality's greatest gift: the freedom to risk everything.

Thalos — Elder fae, wise and weary, father of Kira. Reveals the Law of Exchange and his own survival through the time portal during the ancient eruption. Embodies duty and hidden compassion, his voice carrying the sorrow of generations yet bending toward mercy. Thalos symbolizes endurance and the quiet hope that wisdom can outlast loss. He is proof that living long enough to see your choices come full circle requires both strength and the grace to let go.

Malina — Ancient twin sister to Mahala, granted eternal youth by the same curse that restored her sister's beauty. Haunted by centuries of outliving those she loves—three husbands buried, the newest grave still smelling of fresh-cut stone. Each morning she walks the cemetery paths, fingers brushing headstones, wearing a red scarf she can no longer remove. When Jonas Merrow stumbles into her shop seeking ginger for airsickness, she recognizes grief in him—the lost baby, the wife chasing hope in all the wrong places. She chooses him. Not out of cruelty, but clarity: an end need not be violent to be final. She slips the ancient map into his pocket and whispers, "All treasures are a burden to bear." Later, alone beneath the rising fleet, she releases the weight she has carried for centuries with a prayer: *Let the map reveal what none can find, and the gold that cursed no longer bind.* Malina embodies the danger of living too long—where compassion and despair become indistinguishable, and the kindest act left is letting go.

Mahala — Malina's twin, horrifically scarred by volcanic fire, then cursed with restored beauty and eternal youth in exchange for guarding the temple gold. Bitter and vengeful, she resents her sister's unburned grace and invokes Aelmir to destroy any fleet that steals her treasure. She sees beauty as both gift and prison, despising the pity that once kept her alive. Her wrath fuels the storm, showing how envy and rage can endure longer than love. Mahala is a prisoner of her own making, unable to leave the island that has become her tomb.

Aeronaut Captains and Officers

Captain Von Holt — Captain of the *Nereid*, seasoned aeronaut with a pragmatic streak that borders on ruthless. Values treasure over crew, abandons Aden to his fate on Canyon Myst without hesitation. His greed leads him to prioritize gold over coal, dooming his ship to drift powerless above the Magnetic Sea. When faced with the reality that seven years have passed and his ill wife is likely dead, he steps off the deck into the fog—a final exchange of pride for oblivion. Von Holt becomes a study in how authority corrupted by greed turns survival into betrayal.

Steffan — First mate of the *Nereid*, loyal and competent, caught between following orders and recognizing their doom. Relays the captain's commands even as he watches their choices compound into catastrophe. His silent competence makes him witness to Von Holt's unraveling, a reminder that good men can serve bad captains when duty demands it. Steffan survives to drift on a tomb of gold, his fate unknown.

Kael — First mate of the *Ironwind*, brave and selfless. During the storm, he leaps into the churning sea on a rope to rescue drowning children and survivors, repeatedly risking death while his crew hauls him back from the deep. His actions force the *Ironwind's* captain to dump their entire copper cargo to save the lives Kael pulled from the water. He becomes a symbol of sacrifice and leadership, representing what command looks like when guided by loyalty rather than wealth. His defiance against despair makes him a living legend among sailors.

The Lovers and the Waiting

Mira — Kael's betrothed, auburn-haired and steadfast. Her reunion with Kael after the storm highlights not just relief but the cost of waiting—the terror of watching others return while your beloved's ship remains missing. She is unwavering in love, her relief at his survival tempered by grief for those not spared. Through her, the story shows the silent strength of those who wait on the shore, whose courage is measured not in storms weathered but in hope maintained.

Doran — Storm-worn survivor who returns to Airovale to meet his newborn son for the first time. Rugged and humbled by near-death, he treasures family more deeply than any copper he might have carried home. His quiet scenes with his wife Irina reveal that fortune is measured not in coins but in the faces at his table. Doran stands as a reminder that even hardened men can be reshaped by gratitude, and that coming home is the real treasure.

Irina — Young mother who waited for Doran with their newborn son, initially dreaming of refined dresses and jewelry but transformed by motherhood into someone who values presence over presents. Playful and sharp-tongued, her banter with Doran shows a marriage built on more than wealth. She represents the maturing of desire—from wanting things to wanting time.

Alina — Mother whose husband returns injured and bandaged after the storm. Her small daughter recognizes her father on crutches being helped down the gangplank, and Alina rushes to support them both. They are given a ride home by Kateryna's family, strangers helping strangers. Alina embodies quiet resilience—the strength to hold both hope and fear, relief and exhaustion, in the same moment.

The Seekers of Fortune

Jonas Merrow — Captain of the *Gilded Star*, husband to Sabina. Comes to Malina's shop seeking ginger for airsickness but lingers, hoping for reassurance about the voyage ahead. When he admits they lost a baby—and that this journey is the only thing that excites his wife anymore—Malina slips the ancient map into his pocket unbidden. He startles at her touch, uncertain whether he's been blessed or burdened. His hesitation marks him as a man following his wife's ambition more than his own, hoping treasure might fill the void that grief has carved. Jonas represents the gambler who bets everything on someone else's dream—and must live with where it leads.

Sabina Merrow — Jonas's wife, sharp-eyed and expectant. She waits apart while he fumbles with the healer, her gaze a reminder that hesitation is a luxury they cannot afford. She doesn't ask what the stranger gave him—only raises an eyebrow and says "let's not be late." Her smile is thin, satisfied, the expression of a woman who has already decided what they will find and what it will cost. The loss of their child has hardened something in her; the Crescents offer not adventure but escape from grief she refuses to name. Sabina shows how sorrow can curdle into hunger—and how the sharpest ambitions are often born from wounds that never healed.

The People of Airovale

Garrick Vale — Elara's father, the town quartermaster, aging but sharp. Former aeronaut who flew the Crescents himself and returned "lighter in the hold and heavier in debt." His reflections frame the central parable: *Time is the only treasure; spent by the choices we make.* Became quartermaster to be present when his wife fell ill, finally seeing what he'd missed while chasing winds and wages. His watchful eye on the docks makes him the conscience of Airovale. Through him, the narrative reminds us that the true wealth of a life is measured in what endures when ambition fades.

Elara — Garrick's daughter, meticulous keeper of the quartermaster's ledger. Records every ship, every fee, every departure and return with deliberate precision. She is the symbol of order and inheritance, balancing her father's legacy with her own ambitions. Though distant from the voyages themselves, she dreams of owning airships and making trades—proving herself capable in a world of men. Her presence anchors Airovale as the measure of what is lost and longed for. She represents the next generation, watching the cost of ambition and learning its lessons before taking flight herself.

Kateryna — Farmer's daughter with braids threaded with wildflowers, working the market of Airovale. Inspired by her own family's past hunger, she recognizes the hollow look in Aden's eyes and deliberately chooses him to receive an apple—a gift freely given with the blessing *"na dobro"* (for good). Her brief gesture sets in motion the fortune that directs Aden's path. Later, her family stops to help Alina and her injured husband, offering them a cart ride home. Kateryna embodies the quiet power of kindness, showing how small acts ripple forward in ways we cannot see.

The People of Canyon Myst

Barra — Burly leader of the human settlement on Canyon Myst, betrothed to Kira by arrangement with Thalos. Proud, jealous, and calculating, he sees Kira's defiance as both personal betrayal and political threat to his authority. When publicly humiliated by her rejection and Aden's presence, Barra challenges Aden to a fabricated "duel" to restore his honor. He is the most skilled swordsman on the island but loses control when the crowd begins to favor Aden's mercy. In a final act of murderous rage, Barra throws himself onto Aden's sword while choking him—knowing that his death will trigger the "life for a life" law and doom Aden to execution. His downfall stems from wounded pride, making him a cautionary figure of ambition without humility. In life and death, Barra embodies the cost of control mistaken for love.

Olga — Elderly matriarch of Canyon Myst, frowning and sharp-tongued, who enforces the village's bathing ritual with the authority of a drillmaster. She speaks in a foreign tongue (hints of Slavic roots), barking commands like *"Vso. Davai"* (Everything. Go.) while tossing pumice stones to the bewildered crew. Where Barra brings tension, Olga brings warmth—intimidating in the moment, maternal in purpose. She understands that unwashed strangers attract predators, and will not tolerate filth in her village. After the crew is bathed, clothed, and fed, she takes them into her home—a two-story structure built from living trees and cut timbers connected to the canyon caves—where she sets them up in hammocks with provisions and tools. Her snoring provides cover for Steffan and the others to slip into the jungle that night. Olga represents the practical heart of Canyon Myst: fierce in protection, generous in hospitality, unyielding in standards. She is both gatekeeper and grandmother, embodying the village's strange balance of danger and grace.

Elgin — Fae elder, sharp-tongued and political. Questions Kira's actions and reminds Thalos of the pact's importance, though he once begged Thalos not to take his own daughter instead. Represents the voice of tradition and pragmatism within fae society, challenging decisions even when he knows them to be right. His presence shows that even long-lived beings struggle with hypocrisy and self-preservation.

The Fae Guardian — Unnamed but vital, she is the keeper of sacred sites and mediator between fae and human settlements. Welcomes Kira when she seeks help freeing Aden from prison, and orchestrates the delightful chaos of tiger-assisted distraction that allows their escape. Playful yet dutiful, she represents the younger generation of fae who value friendship and mischief alongside tradition. Her title carries weight and responsibility, but her heart is light enough to give "wedding presents" in the form of enchanted jailbreaks.

Barra's Brother — Younger son with no claim to leadership, yet the one Elgin's daughter chose. Seen in the portal's memory escaping hand-in-hand with her, a generation before the story begins. His family fled not for power but from Barra himself—those closest to him already knowing what he would become. His existence is Barra's deepest wound: proof that even blood saw the monster and ran.

Vivian — Elgin's daughter, the fae princess promised to Barra who refused to endure him. She chose his younger brother instead—a man with no title, no inheritance, nothing but her love—and fled through the portal rather than submit. Her escape left Elgin indebted and silent, and Kira to fill the vacancy. She is the ghost behind Barra's obsession: the first woman who saw him clearly and chose anyone else.

Scelus — Lead guard of Canyon Myst, outwardly loyal to village law but privately aligned with darker plans. Arrests Aden after the duel and closes Barra's eyes with unexpected tenderness, whispering "Farewell old friend, we'll continue what you started." His competence masks ambition. Scelus represents the machinery of power that survives any single leader—patient, watchful, waiting for the next opportunity to advance schemes left unfinished.

Malus — Second in command among the guards, crude and mocking. Takes pleasure in Aden's discomfort during the march to prison, earning a ladle-beating from Olga for his cruelty. Where Scelus calculates, Malus sneers. He is the face of petty authority—dangerous not for his cunning but for his willingness to follow orders without question.

A Final Note on Names

Some characters move through this tale without names attached, not because they lack importance but because they represent all who have stood in their place. The woman who waited at the docks. The child who pointed to the sky. The guard who climbed down from a tree, bewildered by tigers. These are not lesser souls but reflections of the countless lives shaped by the choices of those named above.

In the end, every story is an exchange—memory given for attention, time spent for meaning made. May you spend yours wisely.

About the Author

Jef Gray believes the best stories are the ones we recognize in our own lives.

Born a military brat, Gray attended ten different schools before his high school graduation, never staying anywhere long enough to call it home. That constant motion—the feeling of always arriving, always departing—taught him what aeronauts learn the hard way: that home is people, not places. Years later, as a U.S. Air Force veteran and distinguished technology leader, he watched people make the same wager—trading time for money, working certain hours for uncertain futures.

Airovale was born from a question that haunted him: What if time itself was the treasure we seek, disguised by the pursuits and decisions of the day? Would we later regret chasing wealth over experiences, or find comfort in the fortune we secured?

Gray mixed his interests in art, travel, and science to create a steampunk fantasy world woven from cultures and folklore across an archipelago of volcanic islands—a place where aeronauts fly zeppelins in pursuit of commerce, encounter fae creatures, and make choices paid for by time away from home.

Gray's lifelong fascination with language and culture led him to found the International Peace & Film Festival in 2015, driven by the belief that cultural exchange through art and science can respect borders while building connection for mutual benefit. Participation in the festival, through independent film, has reached 91 countries since it began. That same philosophy runs through *Airovale's* multicultural tapestry—Ukrainian blessings, fae magic, Russian, German, and Irish characters, mixed with American ambition in a world where time is worth more than coin.

When he's not writing, Gray creates micro-documentaries, plays guitar, and spends time with his two children in Orlando, Florida.

www.ingramcontent.com/pod-product-compliance
Lightning Source LLC
Chambersburg PA
CBHW041735300726
48978CB00001B/5